WHEN THE TRUST IS BROKEN

A Novel

Based on real events

Melania Abrams and Maria Testa

TotalRecall Publications, Inc.
1103 Middlecreek
Friendswood, Texas 77546
281-992-3131 TEL
www.mousegate.com

Copyright © 2020 by: Melania Abrams
Copyright © 2020 by: Maria Testa
All rights reserved
ISBN: 9781648830204
UPC: 643977602046
Library of Congress Control Number: 2020939630
Printed in the United States of America with simultaneous printings in Australia, Canada, and United Kingdom.

FIRST EDITION
1   2   3   4   5   6   7   8   9   10

IN MEMORY OF OUR DEAR FRIEND

Table of Contents

Prologue

Every living species has a beginning and an end, that's just the way it is. Some beginnings are quite spectacular with a lot of fanfare, hoop-la and drama. Others are quiet, coming into being in a less auspicious way, hardly making a ripple in an otherwise tumultuous sea of life. The value of a new life is not directly linked to its entrance into this world and special people can appear quietly or with a bang.

Is it merely a twist of fate or a plan outlined by the Almighty that produces a human equipped with higher values and purpose? All of us recognize these individuals, admiring them and quietly wishing we were more like them. Dr. Mary Sliwa, a physician, most frequently referred to, as "Doc" was such a person.

How does one decide the worth of another? Do we not consider kindness, integrity, truthfulness, compassion, empathy, and selflessness honorable virtues? Doc was all of these and more, certainly worthy of our deepest respect. What happened to this good woman can happen to anyone. In this story, you will be present on a journey that reveals how faith in God and trust in true friendship did accomplish the impossible. When injustice is staring us in the face, we must stand up and fight for what is right and just or we will surely fail others and ourselves.

Apathy and silence denying the existence of a wrong will only send a message of approval and increase the likelihood of perpetuating the injustice to others. Bear witness to this story and if you are called upon to advocate for another, realize that with faith and perseverance, what seems impossible can really happen.

CHAPTER 1

Betrayal

Dr. Mary Sliwa trembled as the heavy door closed behind her with a thud. That sound, the finality of it, would remain with her for the rest of her days. What she viewed in those first moments assaulted her memory as she looked to identify her surroundings. Her niece Jean said, "This is your new home, come this way," as she pointed to a plain gray steel door identical to every other gray steel door leading into the patient rooms on this unit. Mary's eyes darted from side to side. The patients here were different; there was a lack of expression on their faces, as they appeared to wander aimlessly past her. In one breathless moment Mary whispered to herself. "My God, this is an Alzheimer unit." This was the first of many thoughts that would tighten her chest and force her pulse to race.

The halls of an Alzheimer unit are always filled with movement as patients walk without any purpose or goal, back and forth between the locked hallway doors oftentimes with the hope of escaping until a staff member redirects them or forces them to rest. Mary Sliwa looked around her and focused on the windowless doors at either end of the long hallway. She watched as people stood at those doors, touched the doorknobs and searched their memories for what to do next. The realization that the doors were locked was wasted on minds that long ago ceased to understand. That reality was not lost on Mary and she screamed inwardly, God help me, I'm in prison.

Mary redirected her focus on Jean as she turned and stepped into the tiny room assigned to her. Her brown oxford shoes offered little noise as she crossed the floor and allowed herself to sink slowly into the familiar brown lazy boy recliner. She rubbed the arms of the chair and realized that this was her chair, the one she rested on daily in her home. How did it get here? When did they move it here? She rested her hands on her knees, leaned back and methodically assessed her surroundings. The one window in the small room was covered with dated flimsy curtains. A white dresser doing double duty as a television stand was positioned beneath. Mary mused at the scratches and chipped paint on the dresser and wondered about all the previous patients that had lived in this room. How did they end up here? Like me, were they virtually kidnapped and plunked down in this place? Continuing on, Mary's eyes settled on the single bed in the corner. There was nothing appealing about it, the cover was nondescript and the one pillow was covered with a pillowcase larger than needed with the open end laying flatly on the bed. A bathroom, awash in white tile with walls that needed a good cleaning and doors that had seen better days, housed a commode and sink. A closet now contained serviceable dark colored sweat pants and sweatshirts not the pastel, crisply ironed blouses and dress pants that hung in the mirrored closet in her home of eight years that had been designed especially for her.

As her anxiety level increased with every thought she reached for the one thing that always brought her comfort, her rosary beads. Holding them and praying the Hail Mary steadied her heart and eased her mind. Soon the quiet ticking of her alarm clock filled the silence in her room.

She thought back to this morning that had begun like any

other with one exception, there was a surprise unscheduled visit by two of her nieces. They promptly extended an invitation to Mary and her sister Rita, to go out for breakfast. They went to one of the local restaurants and had a lovely time and were ready to return home when, Jean, a niece and physician, said that she needed to make a stop at a nursing home to visit one of her patients. She asked Mary to accompany her to the fourth floor. Oddly, there was only a moment when upon entering the Alzheimer unit, Mary had a feeling of impending doom. Before her mind could catch up with her new reality, Jean told her that this was her new home and that she would be safe here. Mary was perplexed. She tried to understand Jean's statement but her brain was not cooperating. Her inability to focus was not new to her. At her last visit to her gerontologist she discussed her lack of focus and recent confusion. The doctor confirmed her suspicions that she most likely was in the early stages of Alzheimer's.

Even with the administration of first-line Alzheimer drug therapy, Mary battled a daily fight to remain in her world. She still remembered that she was Doctor Mary Sliwa and that her friends lovingly called her Doc. She recognized her limitations but she was absolute in knowing that she did not belong in this place.

While Jean arranged Doc's clothes in the shabby dresser, Mary summoned her courage, left the room and eased into the non-ending parade of patients walking in the hallway. As she traveled down the hallway, she noticed each doorway had a picture of a person with their first name to identify them. Some were in wedding clothes from long ago, others stood by themselves at different events in their lives. Strangers, they were all strangers to Mary. The people she passed in the hall never smiled, they just mumbled to themselves and looked totally distracted, even though their pictures all showed them smiling.

The flow of patients that engulfed her led to a fenced in area with artificial trees, park benches and a streetlight, which in its totality gave the appearance of a small park. As Mary got closer to the park area, she passed a room with a window open to the hallway that she quickly identified as the nurse's station. A phone sat on the desk below the window. Mary moved on and sat down on one of the park benches and blended into the surroundings as just another patient while she waited quietly until the nurse's station was empty. Taking advantage of that opportunity, she quickly returned to the window, reached in and picked up the phone. She was familiar with dialing an outside line so she dialed nine and then her friend Stella's number. She was leaning against the wall holding the phone when a nurse approached her and gently took the phone out of her hand as she asked, "Whom are you trying to call?" "My friend," Mary replied with a tremor in her voice. The nurse observed her frightened newly admitted patient and spoke into the phone. She identified herself and the facility and asked, "Who is this?" "This is Stella, Mary's friend," "I've been very concerned about her. Is she being evaluated at the hospital?"

There was a slight pause as the nurse made a critical decision that would remove the cloak of secrecy surrounding Mary's admission. Her eyes fell gently upon Mary and she said, "No, she is a patient in our Alzheimer's unit." Stella's heart skipped a beat as she felt her breath literally freeze in her throat. Wanting to scream at the top of her lungs was her first instinct but she controlled herself, straining to hear everything the nurse was saying. Her mind was racing as she listened, and pieced together,

"Mary's niece brought her to the unit. Mary appears a little confused now but all of this is very new to her." Stella's hand was shaking as she gripped the phone tightly to avoid dropping it. The nurse informed Stella that according to the laws governing patient confidentiality, she could not give her any more information or she would be in trouble.

Stella, a registered nurse assured her that she would never get a fellow nurse in trouble and asked to speak with her friend. When she handed the phone back to Mary the nurse heard her new patient say, "Stella, help me, please. They've put me in prison." Those words and the fear in her patient's voice would haunt the nurse for months to come. She directed Mary back to her room talking to her in soft tones and telling her that everything was going to be ok, but Mary knew better, things would never be the same again.

Back in her room Mary sat amidst Jean's persistent chatter wanting only to be alone and in a quiet space. She willed herself to be calm, closed her eyes and engulfed the memories of her life. Family and friends traversed her mind like the characters on a movie screen. Events that impacted her life for good or bad were drawn together piece by piece. And so she dreamed.

CHAPTER 2

Humble Beginnings

Summer in the bustling garment industry neighborhood in New York was an explosion of noise, with rolling garment racks that careened down the street, and scores of uniformed workers who rushed from one designer house to another. The Sliwa family lived amongst this hustle and bustle. This neighborhood was, for some immigrant families, the first stop on journeys across the country. It was a working-class neighborhood, nothing fancy, just a lot of families struggling to put bread on the table. The Sliwa apartment was nestled on a side street with similar buildings, all with thirteen steps to walk up and front window ledges that supported women of all shapes and sizes who leaned out to shout for their children to come home to dinner.

"Mary, take this lunch pail to your papa please." Anne Sliwa shouted from the apartment stoop. Still in her midwife attire, Anne held the pail out to her youngest child. " All right Mama," replied Mary as she grabbed the pail and started down her street.

This was the best part of Mary's summer days for she relished the time spent with her father. Walking quickly she avoided the cracks in the sidewalk where hundreds of clothes racks had left their mark and made her way to her father's work place. He worked at the Kayser Department Store on Twenty-Second Street and Fifth Avenue, where he was responsible for accepting the delivery of clothing products from textile factories in the Bronx. At this time of the day he was taking his break and young Mary usually delivered her mother's hearty meal to eat.

It was a quick walk and Mary soon stood in front of the side door where the name Kayser appeared in large gold letters. She gave three solid knocks and within a moment the door was opened and her father's face came into focus. "I was beginning to wonder if I would eat today," he said with laughter as he motioned for Mary to step inside." Mary loved seeing her father, his round face, bushy eyebrows and twinkling blue eyes always made her smile.

"I hurried as fast as I could papa." Mary replied, following her father down a small hallway to the back room. She set the pail on a lunchroom table opening it up to let the delicious smells of polish sausage, sauerkraut and freshly baked rye bread escape. He began to eat with gusto and then lifted his eyes looking directly at Mary and asked, "So, what is on the mind of my daughter today?"

He never told Mary how he looked forward to his talks with her, always coming away with a growing respect for her mind. He also held a secret pride in knowing that he was the first one with whom Mary shared her dreams. Looking at her he thought that although she wasn't the most beautiful of his children she was without a doubt the brightest. They conversed in a mixture of Polish, their native tongue, and English. He corrected her Polish and she taught him English and they both laughed at this new language they had somehow developed.

"I was thinking that you and I are very similar when it comes to having a job papa. It seems so logical to me, if we want something or need something, we get a job." The last part she emphasized and her father chuckled. "Yes, I have had many jobs since coming to America. Once I was a barber, another time I worked on the line in a soap factory in the Bronx, and now I work in inventory management for this good store." Mary's eyes settled with pride upon her father. "Papa, did you like all of those jobs?"

"Those jobs gave us the money to survive here Mary. My jobs have been good and gave our family the money needed to live a good life in this country. You and your brothers and sisters will do better. This is why we work hard; to help all our children reach their dreams." Mary thought about that for a moment and then said, "My dreams are always about becoming a doctor and helping people." Her father looked intently at her and thought from where did this one come? Tall and built more like a boy than a girl with a wide smile and thick curly hair, she had a quick mind, a logical mind that was noticed by all. He knew that there would be barriers put up to deter her from her dream, but he also knew that a light burned deeply within her that one day would shine in the world.

"Identity was partly heritage, partly upbringing, but mostly the choices you make in life."
    Patricia Briggs

On the way home Mary considered everything she and her father shared and laughed out loud just thinking of him. He was successful wherever he worked but totally inept at repairing anything in their home. Mary, on the other hand, could always figure out how to fix whatever was broken. Her father would begin the project and then quietly ask Mary to help him finish. He always whispered to her, don't tell your mother. Once, he gave her what he believed was an enormous compliment saying, "You are smart enough to be a man." This further encouraged her curious and analytical mind to tackle any project with success.

The Sliwa's life pretty much mirrored other immigrant families. Everyone was expected to contribute to the general welfare of the family in some way. Mary learned early on that even though she was the baby of the family, there was more expectation placed on her than the others. As she matured she became very inventive when it came to making money. She held a host of jobs in her pursuit of becoming a physician. As a young child, she would do "beer runs" for the men in her neighborhood, taking their beer pails to the local tavern, purchasing beer for twenty cents a pail yet charging each man a quarter, earning five cents' profit on each run. Mary knew the value of money and every little bit helped.

Being tall and large for her age was both good and bad. Her stature helped her land a job running a machine at a fabric factory. She had lied about her age and was able to pull it off until one of the neighborhood men saw her and asked why she was working there since she wasn't yet eighteen. Her boss heard the question and her ability to bring much needed cash into their household came to a quick end.

During high school, she rented a concession stand at local carnivals. She purchased ice cream at the ice cream outlet and sold cones to customers. Eventually, she added cotton candy to her repertoire and boosted her sales.

One job opportunity lasted all of eight hours. She was hired by Macy's and really looked spiffy in her uniform and white gloves. She ran the elevator up and down so many times that it upset her stomach and she threw up. That was the end of her position at Macy's.

If you asked Mary why she became so enthralled with

becoming a physician, something that by all measure should have been out of her reach as a poor woman, she would respond that her yearning to become a physician began while watching her mother practice midwifery, helping to birth babies and tend to the ill. Whenever her mother had a call, Mary would beg to go along. She watched as her mother referred to a book on midwifery and treatment of related ailments, written in her native polish language. Once, her mother found Mary looking at the book and said, "You are too young to be looking at the pictures in this book, they are not meant for young girls." Mary's mind already captured the gist of the images understanding that they were directions on how to help mother's birth their babies, not bad pictures to be kept away from the eyes of a young girl.

Mary witnessed first hand the tenderness of her mother while caring for a woman with burns on her upper body, cleaning and changing the bandages, and experienced the gratitude in the woman's eyes. These experiences combined with her strong faith in God and devotion to the Blessed Mother fueled even more her ambition to become a physician. Her mother acknowledged that desire but warned that she would have to study very hard to do this. Aware of Mary's aspiration her mother knew there was no stopping her. She would become a physician helping others and ultimately lift her family out of poverty.

Mary's mother was probably the greatest influence on her character. From when she was very young her mother encouraged her to study, and used whatever money was available to round out her intellect with music lessons. Mary played the piano, guitar, accordion, trumpet and violin. One instrument, in her hands, literally sang. It was the violin and within a relatively short time she was performing at the church, school functions and even for the Red Cross where her mother was a volunteer. As high school approached, Mary's mother made a decision that would have great impact on Mary. Recognizing her intelligence and drive she decided to send Mary to a private girls school. This was not an easy task for the family, but sacrifice was not new to them. Mary attended Cathedral Catholic high school for girls in Manhattan. It was here that she totally immersed herself in studying and mastering the violin. Those early days were full of learning, working, and helping. Mary helped the family, assisting her parents and babysitting her older sisters' children.

After graduation from high school Mary entered St. John's University in New York City with a bright mind and a strong musical background, having mastered the violin and several other instruments. She was offered and accepted, much to the chagrin of the upper classmen, the first chair in the violin section of the university orchestra. Mary earned her way through the University as she worked two jobs, scrubbing floors at a bank at night and working as a nurse's aide during the day whenever her class schedule allowed.

Upon graduation from college, her mother confided in her that when she became pregnant at the age of forty-six, she knew that her child was destined to be a blessing, not only to her but also to others. She told Mary that God had something special for her to do. Mary reflected on her mother's words and vowed that with God's help, she would make a difference.

One day blurred into the next, always pushing her toward becoming a physician. When it was time to apply to medical school, one of the sisters at her college, Sister Mary, a mentor, urged her to apply to an out-of-state school, telling her that if she remained in the state, her siblings and extended family would not leave her alone, " you have a kind heart Mary, but they are always asking and expecting that you will help them." Mary thought about that and made the decision to apply to Iowa State. She was accepted and began medical school loving every minute of attaining her dream. Unfortunately her love of music and the violin gave way to medicine and from that moment forward the violin remained silent. Mary never forgot what this good sister did for her, and she sent letters and gifts for every occasion and holiday until her mentor passed to the next life.

Life was not easy for a girl who was willing to break societies' norms of becoming a physician. She had few financial resources but her burning desire and courage, coupled with sage advice from mentors such as Sister Mary, pushed her forward. She had such faith in God and herself that as she was graduating from medical school and waiting to take her state board examination, she approached a local banker and applied for a construction loan. Her plan was to include her office and living space for herself and her family. The banker identified Mary as a good prospect and issued the loan. How thrilled she was to take her father to the building with her name on the glass of the front door: Dr. Mary Sliwa. How she wished her mother could have seen her dream come true. Alas, that was not in God's plan, as her mother had died when Mary was in her second year of medical school.

Throughout life, she would often think about her mother's final words to her: "Mary, you are the strong one, promise me you will take care of the family." Mary had promised and stayed true to her word, caring for the entire family at great costs, both financially and emotionally.

CHAPTER 3

Awareness

Mary awoke from her daydreaming as Rita, her sister, entered the room appearing flustered. Rita was a tall lady with gray hair and dark piercing eyes. Along with Mary, intelligence knew no bounds with Rita. She could recall facts about subjects that people had little interest in, but she lacked simple social graces, which led to the belief by many that she was strange. Rita wore her strangeness as a badge of honor; she liked being different and secretly enjoyed her intelligence.

"Mary, I think you'll like it here," Rita babbled as she stood in the middle of the room and turned in a circle, surveying the room. Mary looked at her in total disbelief, shaking her head, asking for God's help "It's God's will Mary, you must make the best of it, " Rita said in her matter of fact manner." "God's will?" Mary knew in the deepest recess of her soul that her God did not will this upon her. Her God was the friend she had kept beside her all these years, the one she talked with, walked with and entreated when she felt lost. No, it wasn't God who placed her here.

Mary pulled her frame up in the chair and emphatically said to all in the room, "Easy for you to say, I don't belong here Rita, I've been kidnapped". An awkward silence descended upon the room. Her words hung in the air for all to see. Kidnapped? That certainly was the appropriate word.

Rita looked upon her sister not quite knowing what to say.

She searched her face and saw such sadness there; it was almost too much to bear. Rita and Mary were more than sisters; they were like two sides of a coin. As Rita grappled with the reality of the situation, Jean began speaking in her clipped, doctor voice, "Kidnapped?" I wouldn't use that term Aunt Mary, we were all concerned about you and wanted you to feel safe and have people around that would help you twenty-four hours a day. This hospital has an excellent reputation, the staff is very professional and the entry and exit doors are totally secure." Mary interrupted her saying clearly.

"Secure entry and exit doors? They are locked Jean, locked! Even I understand what that means. I cannot open them and come and go as I please, I am a prisoner."

The escalation in her voice caused everyone in the room to stop and stare at her. Jean paused putting clothes into the dresser and sat down on the tiny bed. She was dressed in jeans and a sweater, nothing special and certainly did not look like a professional woman. Large dark rimmed glasses framed her brown straight hair and brown eyes. Mary looked across at her and observed the coldness and calculation that had crept into her niece's demeanor. Surely, Mary surmised, Jean must know that I am cognizant of what has transpired with her placing me on this unit. My poor sister must be worried for her own future for if our niece could usurp authority over my life, what could be done to her?

"Those who deny freedom to others deserve it not for themselves"
Abraham Lincoln

Mary made a decision in that moment, going forward, Jean would not be privy to Mary's thoughts. She would be silent and make her plans with the help of God and her good friend Stella. Sitting there as Jean rattled on about visiting the dining room and seeing what was prepared for lunch, Mary's thoughts were categorizing what Jean had implemented. It was apparent that Jean had disregarded Mary's legal living trust, a document that Mary had prepared years before with her lawyer which codified her wishes, that if she became disabled or ill, if feasible she wished to remain in her home with a caretaker. Mary had amassed sufficient funds in her working life to provide for herself and Rita as they aged. Mary was now eighty years old and her sister was eighty-five. She was aware now that following her previous fall, stroke, and fractured hip; Jean's push to become her guardian was just the beginning of the plan to bring her here. Jean had told Mary that guardianship was a perfunctory process so that she could help her pay bills, and take better care of her and her sister, but Mary discovered, with her incarceration, that this was a lie. Mary remained quiet and did not converse with Jean. The silence in the room was suddenly broken when Stella and her daughter Anne, knocked on the door. Stella had received the call from Mary and believed her friend was in trouble. She came as quickly as possible seizing the opportunity to help her friend. Jean stared at Stella in total disbelief. This definitely was not in the plan. Jean had gone to great lengths to keep this plan a secret, but Stella had found her friend and far sooner than Jean ever expected.

Mary turned towards the door. The light in the short hallway was dim but as she focused a smile began to engulf her face. There stood Stella, her trusted friend. Mary 's relief and joy was as apparent as the redness that began to creep up Jean's neck and face. Jean was uncomfortable to say the least both with the fact that Stella had found her friend so quickly and with the obvious disdain that Mary had directed toward her. She wanted to run from the room but Stella was blocking the doorway. Rita kept repeating,

"Oh how did you know we were here? I'm so glad to see you and I know my sister is happy." Jean then did the only thing available to do. She abruptly stood and with a sharp edge to her voice issued a directive to Rita. "Rita It's time to go, we'll come back tomorrow." Rita appeared confused as she was ushered from the room and said with her back to Mary, "I'll be back, I love you."

The door closed and silence surrounded the remaining three. Joy now turned to sadness as Stella and her daughter moved to embrace Mary. Stella's daughter Anne picked up Mary's hand holding it tightly. Anne was visibly shaken because she, like her other siblings, loved this woman who had become an integral part of her mother's life and theirs as well. Anne was a professor at the local New York University satellite site and taught art and film to eager students. She was rarely out of the teaching mode and could readily explain just about anything to anyone. But, in this instance, her mind was drawing a blank. There was no explanation available and she was distraught. As her mother sat down on the bed opposite Mary's chair, Anne moved to the window allowing two good friends to attempt to piece together this new reality.

"Doc, how on earth did this happen?" Stella asked, using Mary's nickname. Doc looked at her with tears forming in the corner of her luminous brown eyes. "Stella, it all happened so quickly. Rita and I were at home when our nieces Jean and Betty appeared at the door. They surprised us and had come to invite us out to breakfast. It seemed to be a lovely idea.

On the way home Jean told me that she wanted to visit one of her patients and asked if I would like to accompany her. One minute I was eating waffles and ice cream and next walking through that gray door at the end of the hall. There was such a loud, final sound as it suddenly closed behind me.

The pitiful look upon her face spoke volumes, looking as she had aged ten years in just a day. Her voice quivered and she shook slightly as she expressed the horror of what was now surrounding her. "My God Stella, have you seen the poor souls walking in the hallway?"

Please don't let me end my days here among people who are lost in their minds. I'll go crazy."

Stella's head was spinning; it was so difficult trying to make sense out of what had happened. All she could say was, "Try and be calm Doc, I'll be back tomorrow and we'll talk."

People have been placed against their will into asylums by crazed relatives or spouses, but Doc's placement by her niece, herself a physician, didn't make sense. In the back of Stella's mind a sinister plot came into focus. It was now evident that a myriad of lies had been told in order to provide the appropriate criteria for Doc's admission to the locked Alzheimer unit. Stella wondered if all of this preparation was done to negate any possibility of Doc's being cared for at home, which would have followed the directions of the living trust. Flashes of Doc's kindness towards her niece Jean rushed forward through Stella's memory. There were so many events to consider.

Jean was the first child born to Doc's eldest sister Sylvia who was now deceased. Since Jean was the first niece Doc felt a special bond with her. Doc doted on all of Sylvia's children but especially on Jean. It wasn't just that Doc paid for Jean's college and medical school but she even purchased a new car for her, ensuring that she had safe and reliable transportation to school.

Doc continued to recount how she felt she was hoodwinked into entering the nursing home. Shaking her head, she was obviously distraught over what had transpired. "She lied to me!" exclaimed Doc."

It was obvious that she was becoming more agitated so Stella spoke slowly and gently repeating that she would return the next day. Words seemed unnecessary as Stella and Anne left Doc's room. Exiting through the gray door they walked in silence to the elevator. Funny, this side of the building had an entirely different look. A bulletin board was situated across from the elevator that welcomed visitors and had announcements of upcoming events. Birthdays were highlighted with the staff members picture and good wishes from all. As they rode down the elevator, Stella and Anne would recall that all seemed surreal. They walked and talked but everything else was foggy as if in another dimension. Exiting the building, their eyes were drawn up toward Doc's room, which overlooked the parking lot. There she stood, with one hand on the glass window and the other waving a large tissue box. Tears flowed unceasingly down Stella's face. She brushed them away, waved back, threw a kiss, and smiled at her dearest friend. In that instant, something deep within Stella began to form.

CHAPTER 4

The Plan

Once home, Stella moved through the house and aimlessly picked up small bits of clutter. Simple tasks helped her to get from one moment to the next without continually crying. She teetered between hysteria and exaggerated control every time her thoughts drifted to Mary or Doc, as she always referred to her. She and Doc were close, so tied together in friendship that Stella knew exactly what Doc was experiencing.

Stella had so many thoughts whirling around in her brain that it was difficult to focus. She had that look on her face that prompted those who had worked for her to remark, ' Stand back, she's on a roll!' Stella was beautiful in her own way. She had that put together look while working as a hospital's vice president of patient care services, always in suits, heels and favorite pieces of jewelry. Her piercing brown eyes flashed behind glasses rimmed with a delicate golden thread. If you were to ask people what they remembered most about Stella, they would say, her smile. That smile was disarming and known to neutralize the fiercest of foes from wildly out of control surgeons to chief financial officers who questioned her numbers. Brushing her shortly cropped curly brown hair away from her forehead, she stretched out her five foot eight inch slender frame across the sofa and forced herself to calm her brain. Stella had always been able to sift through problems and find a solution, but what Doc experienced bordered on being kidnapped and what would that solution look like? The situation involved other people and was out of Stella's control. She felt hopeless and unable to intercede to help her friend.

To control her anxiety, she practiced breathing exercises and eventually modulated her respirations and could think clearly. Her thoughts flowed back to how she and Doc became friends. Stella had been aware of Doc as she was the president of the medical staff but it was at the opening of their new hospital where this female doctor gave the invocation that Stella was truly impressed. Looking everyone directly in the eyes she spoke simple words of truth and identified goals and ambitions. Anyone listening to her words that day had to have experienced the pride in her voice to be opening a hospital that was committed to doing good in the community. That was Doc in a nutshell thought Stella. It was never about her, it was always about others and how she, with God's grace would help them.

Stella remembered the first time she was able to speak with Doc. They were seated next to each other at a hospital committee meeting where Stella, who always enjoyed jewelry, noticed a college ring upon Doc's finger and inquired about it. "That's a unique looking ring." Doc was proud to tell her," This is my St. John's College ring." "Oh, my goodness, one of my daughters attends St. John's." She looked with interest at this woman who was always quietly in control of all situations. She appeared to know everybody in the room and they knew her deferring to her wisdom often throughout meetings. "You've picked a very good school; the Sisters are excellent teachers."

During their conversation before the meeting began they formed a connection because they had both recently built new homes. Doc's home was close to the hospital in an upscale neighborhood and Stella's was twenty minutes away in Queens. Stella was laughing, saying, "My yard is a total mess. I had to hire a crew to come in and grade everything to make it level. I didn't have any extra money for sod so I also had them seed the entire yard." Doc thought about the fact that her landscaping had already been completed, but she didn't mention it so as not to make Stella feel uncomfortable. Instead she said, "I'm not sure I know where you live in Queens." This gave Stella the opportunity to write out her address, giving it to Doc. "I'll be home this weekend, if you're available and in the area, feel free to stop in."

The following weekend, Stella's brother in law, Sam arrived at her house for coffee and gossip walking across the yard and hoping to play a couple rounds of pinochle with Stella. He was married to Marie, Stella's sister but Stella and her children couldn't help but love him as well. He was a complex character, tall, strong, and handsome with a robust laugh and willing spirit. When responding to questions, he spoke clearly and from his heart. Stella and Sam were playing cards when the doorbell rang. Stella rose and went to the front door and there stood this unassuming physician with a very large bottle of Cutty Sark in her hands. Stella would find out years later that Doc was regifting the bottle since she only drank Chivas Regal. "I was in the neighborhood," Doc said with a grin. Stella introduced Sam to Doc as they walked towards the kitchen. Sam usually had little regard for physicians saying, "we have to address them as doctor so-and-so, nobody addresses me as mechanic Sam." He soon learned that this doctor was different. Maybe it was because they were both from the same era that they understood one another so well, unlike Stella who was thirteen years younger. Doc and

Sam went on to become friends and eventually physician and patient.

From the first time Doc stood at her door Stella was extra mindful of this unique physician who chided her fellow physicians whenever they criticized the nursing staff. Doc's response to their complaints was, "Where would you be without the nurses? Are you at the bedside at three in the morning?" One moment, one statement, one turn of events, can totally change the direction and intent of one's life. Beginning to know Doc was Stella's moment.

"A faithful friend is the medicine of life"
Ecclesiasticus, 6:16

Doc and Stella became each other's faithful friend. As their lives intertwined, Doc included Stella with the rest of her friends who loved visiting Savannah, Georgia, especially in the cold winter months. They usually patronized the casino to gamble but mostly they would laugh and enjoy themselves. Stella was usually with them. In thinking back, she could see in her mind's eye how their friendship grew and solidified with trust as the glue. Twenty years later when Doc was looking to sell her home, it was Stella that told her that the empty lot next to her own was soon to be for sale. Stella lived in Queens off of two hundred-sixty first Street having purchased the home twenty years previously at a really good price. Doc liked where Stella lived and proceeded to buy the available lot, built a beautiful home and moved in bringing her sister Rita with her.

Stella's reminiscing was interrupted with the barking of Anne's dog, Ginger, who wanted to be let out. Stella walked to the door and realized that, just as a dog barks, she must find her voice and not be quiet about Doc's incarceration. Verbalizing her thoughts, she ran through a list of tactics that usually brought her success and began to create a plan. The plan included an intensive review of what had transpired since Doc's fractured hip two years ago and the involvement of Doc's family at a level not seen before. She realized that the first stage of the plan already existed, for Stella had begun to journal following the fall that fractured Doc's hip. For Stella, the journal was a means of coping. It combined her 'nursing mode' and her obsessive-compulsive trait to meticulously document everything. The journal included general notes of improvement and notes describing Doc's family's unusual participation in her care.

CHAPTER 5

The Journal

Based on Stella's notes

Thursday of the first weekend in December arrived with a brief snowfall and a plunge into a freeze that allowed ice to form in patches over the streets and walkways. Stella had prepared to join two other friends for their annual holiday weekend away to upper state New York where small towns ablaze with Christmas decorations and unique shops abounded. It was late afternoon and the sun had already begun to dip below the horizon when Doc stepped outside her front door and started down the steps. She was going next door to Stella's house as she had a thousand times before to visit with Stella and Anne. Doc didn't see the thin sheath of ice lurking at the edges of the stairs and lost her footing, falling hard against the cement steps. She was in tremendous pain and lay there for a while before maneuvering herself into position to reach her cell phone pocketed in her jacket to dial Stella's phone number.

Stella would never forget that call or the look of anguish on her friend's face as she and her daughter rushed next door. With one look at the position of Doc's left leg she knew that her hip was broken. "Anne, go to the house and grab that cover off the sofa." Her words were no sooner out of her mouth and Anne was home, retrieved the cover and was back wrapping Doc securely in the blanket. The ambulance with its flashing lights arrived sliding and jerking to the right due to the ice encrusted street before it stopped in front of Doc's home. Two paramedics emerged and quickly assessed Doc's situation. They were all business as they asked Doc questions, listened to her rendition of what happened, made their determination and gently secured her to a board limiting her left hip from movement. "I'm going to go with you in the ambulance Doc." Stella waited for the paramedics to lift Doc up into the ambulance and then climbed on board thankful that she could be with her friend. The ride was loud and bumpy and Doc appeared very uncomfortable murmuring," God help me, God help me," Stella silently prayed over and over to keep Doc safe and heal her. She reassured herself that Doc was a strong person and would be able to come through this. She was already mentally preparing herself to help her. Stella reached for her phone fumbling from one pocket to another as she rarely placed it back in the same space. She placed two calls, one to Dr Pilano, Doc's friend and physician and one to Jean, Doc's niece "Jean, its Stella, Doc has fallen and it appears that she may have broken her hip. I'm in the ambulance with her and we are on our way to Montefiore Medical Center. I've already spoken to Dr. Pilano who said she'd meet us there. Is there anyone else I should call?" "Not at this point Stella, I'm still seeing patients and will meet you at the hospital as soon as I can."

When Stella and Doc arrived at the hospital Dr. Pilano was standing in the ambulance bay. She was an unassuming individual who had first trained as a nurse and then followed Doc's advice to go into medicine. They were friend's first and then practitioners. She brushed her blond hair away from her eyes and with it a few tears when she saw her friend in painful distress. Stella stood for a moment after exiting the ambulance and watched while they ushered Doc into the first cubicle across from the nurse's desk. Stella being a registered nurse knew the drill and remained in the waiting area to allow the staff to make decisions without interruption. It didn't take very long. The emergency room physician reviewed x-rays and made the diagnosis of a fractured hip. Doc was admitted to the hospital to await surgery the next day.

Stella struggled inwardly with the diagnosis and impending surgery because she fully understood the risks associated with a hip repair on a woman Doc's age. When Jean arrived, Stella approached her and said, "What would you think about having one of us stay twenty-four-seven with Doc so that she will see familiar faces?" Jean shook her head in agreement, "I'll arrange my schedule to be here at night if you can take the daytime." There was a flurry of activity with Jean, the emergency room physician and orthopedic surgeon huddled together as they looked at Doc's x-rays and weighed the pros and cons of treatment. They informed Doc about the result of her x-ray and proposed a plan of treatment. Doc agreed that a repair must be done but seemed nervous about the prospect of surgery. Maybe it was the drugs used to suppress her pain or perhaps all the strangers that flooded her room that caused Doc to stammer and prompted Stella to say, "Doc, I am so sorry that this has happened to you." Doc looked up at her friend and reached out for her hand. If Stella could read her friend's eyes, they clearly said, "I'm afraid, Please stay with me." Responding to this Stella lingered until Doc was given medication for pain and Jean had settled in to spend the night with her. As she slipped out of the room her friend's eyes were shut in restful sleep and she held fast to the medal hanging around her neck.

Later at home Stella suffered through a fitful night. Between bathroom runs and checking the clock there was little time left for solid sleep. Finally, Stella gave in, turned on the light and pulled her rosary out of the bedside stand to pray that Doc would have a successful surgery and recovery. Around five thirty she arose and drew the bedroom curtains aside to see snow falling in a steady stream. The streetlight's yellow cone of light illuminated the sidewalk where fluffy layers of white accumulated. Stella made the bed, showered and dressed herself in khaki pants with a light brown v-neck sweater. She quietly descended the stairs and entered the kitchen. Anne had left the coffee pot ready to be plugged in and there was an assortment of sliced coffee cake on a plate with a note, "For you!" God bless her daughter, always thinking of ways to help her.

The hospital at seven a.m. was bristling with activity. Fresh faces peeked out of hooded winter coats still dusted with patches of snow as they rode the elevators to their assigned units with lunch bags in hand. White coats crowded around nursing stations, stethoscopes hanging precariously from pockets or strung unceremoniously around necks, as the plan for the day was discussed. Stella moved through this familiar scene to the private room assigned to Doc on the unit. She washed her hands with the alcohol-based cleanser and opened the door. Jean was talking on her cell phone as Stella entered and turned away from her covering the phone with her hand. Stella caught the tail end of the conversation "we'll have to assess that as she is recovering, for now, we'll put off any decision for a later date." Stella approached Doc's bedside and said, Good morning Doc." There was no response, her eyes were shut and she appeared to be in a deep sleep, gently snoring. Stella rubbed her friend's arm with still no response. "I know I can be a worry wart but something is wrong, Doc doesn't seem to be responding as she should. What do you think Jean?" "Well, she's on some heavy-duty pain killers and relaxants, I think its just the medication. I'll be back tonight before Doc's scheduled surgery. Has the nurse been in to evaluate Doc?"

As if on cue, the nurse came in to monitor Doc's vital signs and Stella approached her saying, "Doc doesn't seem to be responding, I can't seem to arouse her, have you noticed this as well?" "She is on some pretty strong medication, I'm sure that accounts for some of her stupor."

Continuing to attend to her patient, the nurse did a short assessment to measure Doc's alertness but could not get her to open her eyes or speak. Stella instinctively knew that something was very wrong.

Waiting until Jean left for the day, Stella proceeded to do her own assessment of Doc. She lifted each of Doc's arms independently and allowed them to fall back. Stella noted that Doc's right arm fell in a flaccid pattern. From her years of working as a registered nurse she suspected that Doc had suffered a cerebral vascular accident or stroke. She pushed the nurse call light and said to the nurse attending Doc, "I've done my own assessment of my friend's alertness and honestly I believe something is not right, I think she's experienced a stroke." The nurse responded, "I'll page the resident on call right away."

Doc did not awaken throughout the day and still no one agreed with Stella's suspicions. Her concern was becoming palpable and confirmed when, in the early evening Doc was transported to the operating room where the anesthesiologist spoke to Jean saying, "Your Aunt appears to have sustained a cerebral vascular accident. I am not recommending surgery without further evaluation."

At that point, Jean, who, in Doc's living trust was identified as the medical power of attorney, intervened and made the decision to allow the surgery to go forward, even with the heightened risk. Stella was grateful that the decision was not hers to make. Doc's niece made the right call. That evening was difficult to endure knowing that Doc was in such a fragile state and realizing that without the hip repair she could be a permanent invalid. Stella prayed to everyone she could remember who left this earth in good faith that Doc would make a good recovery. It didn't hurt that this was December eighth a Holy Day in the Catholic Church honoring the Immaculate Conception of the Virgin Mary to whom Doc always prayed.

After surgery and once Doc opened her eyes, Stella's anxiety level began to decrease. Doc was unable to speak clearly and kept repeating, "Oh well, oh well" over and over again, but, she could move her right side without problems even though her left appeared very weak. Stella knew the tenacity of her friend and felt this function would return. The initial days in the Intensive Care Unit included having Doc receive the Catholic blessing of the sick not once but three times due to Stella's miscommunication. At one point, Doc must have wondered, what in the world she had done wrong to warrant three blessings? Stella smiled and mused that Doc probably questioned if any of them really knew what they were doing, but accepted it since nothing was better in her mind than prayers. Doc's recovery progressed and eventually she was discharged to a rehabilitation center.

One has to wonder how difficult this whole process must have been for Doc. She was a physician who was used to writing the orders for her patients, consoling them as they attempted to speak and holding their hands as they cried. Now she was that patient, needing assistance in feeding, bathing, going to the bathroom, and performing the bedside exercises left by the physical therapy staff. Stella was determined to do everything possible to help her friend. She arrived at rehab every day at lunchtime and remained there until Doc's eyes were closed in sleep.

The holidays approached and Doc's wish to be home for Christmas materialized. Since she was still limited in being able to function on her own and needed continued therapy, Stella offered her home to her and brought her there. Home care was arranged and soon staff proficient in speech, occupational, and physical therapy came on a regular basis. Within a short period of time, Doc was well on her way to full recovery.

During this time, Doc celebrated her eightieth birthday and Stella and her daughter Anne invited many of her family and friends to join them for a party at their home. Anne provided a beautiful dinner and delicious delights for dessert. Doc appeared to be enjoying herself and although her speech was slurred everyone understood what she had to say. During the festivities Doc's niece Betty delivered a very public message to Stella and her family saying, "Thank you Stella and Anne for all of the love and attention you have showered on our aunts Doc and Rita. It is profoundly appreciated."

Stella noticed that Betty didn't look at her or Anne but was raising her glass and toasting towards Jean. There was something odd in Betty's voice that stirred an uncomfortable feeling in Stella. Betty, the niece not especially liked by Doc because of her past inappropriate statements regarding Doc, her money, and her possessions, always seemed to be calculating, looking for an opportunity to benefit herself. Stella from the time she was little truly had a sixth sense that developed as she aged. People or events could trigger that sense and would alert her to look at what is not apparent to the naked eye. During this time, she could see the storm clouds gathering.

The first lightning bolt struck within the week when Jean, out of the blue, said to Stella, "I've hired a caretaker to take care of Doc and Aunt Rita. I know this is going to be difficult because Doc does not like strangers in her home but I'm convinced that they need someone twenty-four seven to care for them?" "Well, I can understand that, who did you hire?" "It's Beth," said Jean." Stella knew Beth was the ex-wife of Jean's brother. Jean was downright bubbly and excited about the prospect of a caregiver and happy that it was someone she knew well.

Actually this will help Beth in other ways. Since her divorce from George she has decided to put her house on the market and it needs to be painted inside and out so she was looking for a place to rent while the work is being done. So this sort of helps us both, she has a place to stay with her family and I have someone to watch Doc and Rita."

Stella, in looking at the selection of a caretaker was dismayed as she was aware that Beth, even though she was divorced from George was still part of the family dynamics and her sixth sense kicked in as she wondered if there were other motives involved in her caring for Doc. Beth did not come alone, her daughter Carol, a college student also stayed in the house. Jean thought this was the perfect solution for someone to be there twenty-four seven to care for Doc and Rita. The arrangement was far from a solution. Doc was used to a peaceful environment with predictable routines. She was now made to endure loud voices and music from people who were nearly strangers to her. Also, as Beth, a registered nurse, worked at the hospital three days a week, arrangements had to be made for who would be the caretaker of Doc and Rita for those days. A nephew was enlisted to sit in the house but spent most days sleeping on the couch. Stella wondered who indeed was benefiting from this arrangement, Doc or Beth? Doc seemed to be on the short side of the agreement since Beth wasn't the ideal care provider Jean needed. She fell short on many fronts, especially in providing healthy meals, as her idea of breakfast was a sweet roll and dinner, pizza. It was a constant struggle for Doc to maintain her independence and eventually she showed signs of frustration with the situation.

Toward the end of February, Stella, her sister with her husband Sam and Doc traveled to Stella's second home in Savannah, Georgia. Stella's son Michael purchased the condo and generously gave it to her, saying, 'You and your friends will enjoy this.' What a God send that place became. Doc was happy there and was able to include runs to physical and speech therapy with trips to the casino. She improved in her walking, speaking, and playing bingo. Stella's friends from home and Savannah visited and encouraged Doc to speak. Her friends were also nurses and knew Doc experienced a form of aphasia so when she inserted the wrong word or repeated an inappropriate phrase, they just made light of it and would get her to laugh at herself teasing her to continue. They all remarked at how well she was doing. As they were preparing to return home, Doc told Stella "This is heaven for me, how I wish I could stay here in Savannah." "Me too Doc, me too."

On Easter Sunday, Stella walked across the yard separating

her home and Doc's to wish her friend and her family a blessed Easter. After ringing the doorbell, Jean appeared and pulled the door open with obvious hostility. There was a sour look upon her face.

"Happy Easter Jean." came from Stella's lips but her greeting fell on deaf ears. Stella was dumbstruck. She didn't consider her a friend but certainly they were always respectful of each other. Jean's response to Doc's fall and ultimate stroke initially was that of a caring niece. Something obviously had occurred during Stella and Doc's trip to Savannah and Jean was unable to mask her displeasure with Stella. Her face was encased in accusatory anger and Stella felt the rage engulf her. Stella quickly assessed recent events, trying to figure out what caused this change but nothing came to mind. She stepped into the front hallway and saw many of Doc's family in the living room. "Happy Easter everyone." Some of them responded with the same phrase but Betty, Jean's sister looked straight at Stella with disgust in her eyes. "May I see Doc?"

Stella was being physically blocked by Jean's presence in the hallway and didn't want to just brush past her and enter Doc's bedroom. "She's sleeping and shouldn't be disturbed." Jean announced. Stella could hear Doc calling her name from the bedroom. Not wanting to make a scene, she said she would return later when Doc was awake. As she left Doc's house, Stella experienced an overwhelming jolt of anxiety. She had heard her friend calling her name, saying, "I'm here" and she felt that she was abandoning her.

Easter was just the beginning of the strange things that happened that spring. A spiderlike web began to form with Stella as the target in the middle. No matter what Stella and Doc planned, a sinister wickedness emanated from Jean and Beth. During this time Stella searched her mind and looked for any clue to help her understand this dramatic change in Jean.

Stella indulged Doc whenever possible as it gave her pleasure to help her friend. One of those pleasures involved playing bingo at the local churches. Doc had both simple tastes and simple pleasures. It wasn't just that she liked to play the game; she prided herself on knowing the players, on kidding with them, on inquiring about their families and themselves. Everybody knew Doc, greeting her in one voice when she walked in: "Hi, Doc!" Beth did not like taking her to bingo and Stella, because of her asthma, had to avoid too much smoke. Stella found a church property that was smoke-free and on most Mondays they would enjoy the evening playing bingo. One Monday, returning home around 10:30 pm, Stella walked Doc into her house. She had noticed Jean's car parked in front and wondered, given the hour if she was staying over. As they entered the foyer, they heard voices from the kitchen. Jean, Rita and Beth were seated at the kitchen table. Jean raised her eyes to Stella and then dropped them immediately to her hands crossed on the table. Stella helped Doc to her bedroom and was leaving when Jean said, "I'd like to speak with you privately." Her tone was one that a principal would use with an errant student. "Sure" Stella replied as she opened the front door.

Later, Stella would express that a chill ran up her spine as she noted that Jeans behavior and tone of voice seemed to have all the earmarks of a moment when life changes abruptly. Stella stepped down to the third step and turned to face Jean standing on the top step. Jean had assumed an authoritative stance as she towered over Stella. The conversation that ensued was about something supposedly overheard by Carol, Beth's daughter, when Stella picked up Doc for bingo. Jean said, "Carol has reported that when you came to pick up Doc you loudly complained about how dirty the house is and what poor care Doc and Aunt Rita are receiving." Jean's face said it all. She was nearly breathless as she angrily went on about demeaning the help that she had hired to care for her aunts.

"Why would I say something about Carol and Beth knowing I would be overheard? I was very aware that Carol was in her room and wasn't more than fifteen feet away and could hear everything we said. Our conversation was not about the two of them. Please ask Carol to come out so I can clear this up?" "That's not going to happen as Carol is studying for her final exams. This conversation is over." Jean huffed, turned and with great disdain walked back into the house.

Stella believed she made a tactical error that night. She should have re-entered the house and addressed Carol directly but that was not her style and she didn't want to upset Doc. Later, she wrote a detailed letter to Jean, Beth, and Carol, requesting a meeting to clear up some of the misconceptions. She received no reply. Stella now was suspicious that there was more behind the change in Jean's demeanor than a simple misunderstanding. She took a brief, planned trip to Savannah. Shortly after her return Jean and her daughter Beverly paid her a surprise visit. Stella answered the door with a smile. "Hello Jean, Beverly" Stella was taken back that they were at her home, but always being a gracious host, she invited them in. Jean, who had been in her home on several occasions, breezed right past her and into the kitchen. She slammed down a recorder onto the table, removed her trench coat and seated herself as if court was about to be in session. Stella asked Beverly to make herself comfortable. "You won't mind if I record this," Jean said haughtily as she set up the recorder and was about to begin when Stella responded, "I most certainly do mind if you record whatever will transpire here and may I ask why you think this is necessary?" Stella's voice was measured and quiet as it always was when she was controlling her emotions. "It is for your benefit to understand what is said," Jean spoke while Stella shook her head and asked, "How does that benefit me since you are the one who will have the recording?"

The situation was becoming unbearable with Jean staring at Stella and Stella unwaveringly returning her gaze. Silence spoke loudly in the room. Finally, Stella said, "Since you think I am not capable of understanding a conversation, I will call my sister to come over and interpret for me."

During the wait for Marie who lived next door, Stella attempted many times to engage Jean in conversation but to no avail. After Marie arrived, Jean announced. "You are no longer allowed to pay Doc's bills or handle any of her affairs. Instead, I will be in charge as Doc has been declared incompetent." Stella looked at her sister Marie who appeared to be in shock. She drew in a sharp breath wondering how Jean could speak with such disrespect about her aunt, mentor, supporter, and benefactor. It was frightening how an eleven-lettered word, incompetent, could strip away a person's dignity, possessions, and friends, essentially an entire life. Worse, it fell off Jean's tongue with such ease. Jean continued, I am in possession of a copy of Doc's trust that names me as power of attorney." "I have no problem with that but again, why did you feel it was necessary to record this conversation?" asked Stella as she held her growing disdain for

Jean in check. Jean exasperated at this point admitted that it was her attorney who suggested recording the conversation to make sure that Jean's implementing her Power of Attorney responsibilities were clearly understood by Stella. Jean went on to explain that she was now aware that Stella was in the trust and would receive the house. Stella responded in a calm, firm voice," "I have been a true and loyal friend to Doc and do not deserve this treatment from you." It was now very apparent to Stella that Doc's many stories of how her family had misused her for financial reasons were true. Marie, who had remained silent through most of the exchanges, spoke up.

"You know Jean, my sister and your aunt have developed a trust and friendship that we all could admire. While Doc was in Savannah, she took her to her daily therapy sessions leaving the house at seven am. She never once complained and I must add that Doc looked cleaner, happier and certainly more presentable under her care than with Beth." Judging by Jean's face, Marie's words were not accepted well.

Stella who had recovered from her initial anger was in full attack mode. "Since you are now in charge of everything, you should be aware of a phone call I received from Liza, Doc's financial advisor." This grabbed Jean and she responded with tight lips and eyes filled with hate. Stella had met Liza at their local bank as Stella was helping Doc consolidate and manage her investments. Doc purchased stocks but had little interest in managing them. Liza was a god-send as she put everything into order and frequently came to visit Doc to go over her portfolio. In time, she became Doc's friend and gained Stella as a client. "Someone was attempting to assign themselves as the principal owner of Doc's investments", Stella said, "Do you know anything about that?" Jean blatantly denied any knowledge, but Stella already knew that Jean was the person who attempted to change the ownership of Doc's investment accounts. Over the years, Liza observed Doc and Stella's friendship and was aware of Doc's gradual decline. What Jean did not know was that Liza also had a copy of Doc's trust in her file. So when Jean presented Doc's sister, Rita, to the financial advisors' desk and inquired about removing Doc's name on her accounts and establishing Rita as the sole owner, Liza was naturally suspicious. Stella supposed Jean thought that it would simplify her ability to have free access to Doc's money. Jean claimed that it was Rita who had invested the money into Doc's investments and that since Doc was no longer capable, it would be easier to administer the accounts if everything was in Rita's name. Liza questioned Rita "Is this true?" According to Liza, Rita looked at her niece Jean before answering and said, "Jean what did you want me to say?" Liza told Stella that it was glaringly evident that Jean's surreptitious actions had been found out. She saw that nothing was going to change and left the bank with Rita in tow.

"Jean, you should be aware that I instructed Liza to follow the bank's policy on a potential fraudulent act." With that, Jean, aware of Stella's assistance to Doc regarding payment of bills etc, stood and motioned to her daughter to get up saying to Stella. "I will need whatever papers and documents you have in your possession related to Doc's finances, as soon as possible." They were headed for the front door when Stella responded, "I'll gather them, but if you recall I have already given you a list of all of Doc's financial investments and accounts after Doc's fall and stroke."

Stella always had important papers and documents in order

but she delayed handing them over to Jean until she could contact her personal attorney regarding the legality of everything Jean was attempting to do. Stella was convinced that Jean was executing a plan to eliminate her from her friend's life.

After Jean's exit, Stella reviewed in her mind everything that had been said. It now seems perfectly clear that during Doc and Stella's trip to Savannah, the living trust kept in Doc's office at home was discovered. It was obviously read by Jean and others living in Doc's house. It must have been highly disturbing to Jean as she assumed that the family would benefit from Doc's passing as they had always benefitted from her generosity. Stella could see that Jean jumped to many conclusions regarding her involvement in Doc's finances. If she had only asked Stella prior to the meeting she would have gladly shared all the documentation she kept as a matter of course, such as cancelled checks, bank accounts, and receipts. Stella was convinced that Jean thought that she had misappropriated Doc's money but nothing could be further from the truth. Prior to Stella assisting Doc with her bills, it was evident that bills were not being paid on time. Doc had asked Stella to help her. They worked out a system where Stella reviewed the bills with Doc and wrote the checks and Doc signed them. Thinking back, Stella remembered when this failure in Doc's memory was foretold. Five years prior, Stella went with Doc to a gerontologist who had her tested for memory loss. This physician knew of Doc and her work and as she was leaving, the physician embraced her and thanked her for paving the way for women now in medicine. Weeks later when they returned for the test results, Doc sat expressionless while the physician told her that she likely was in the early stages of Alzheimer's or some form of dementia but added that, because of her level of intelligence, her cognitive reserve would delay the progression of the disease. On the ride home Stella didn't know what words to use to help Doc with such discouraging results but it was Doc consoling Stella saying, "I'm going to leave everything in God's hands."

Doc was at Stella's home the morning following Jean's unannounced visit. After offering coffee and donuts to Doc, Stella sat and went over what Jean had said regarding Doc's trust in her mind. She had to take her at her word since Stella had never seen the final version of Doc's Trust. And, there was no need to see the trust until now. "Doc, do you recall making any changes to your original trust?" Stella asked as she poured another cup of coffee. "I can't recall any right now," Doc said reaching down to pet Anne's dog that eagerly awaited her touch. "If it's okay with you Doc, I will call the attorney who drew up your trust and have him forward a copy to you." "It's ok, I'd like to review it one more time as well."

Stella sipped her coffee as she contacted the attorney. She sat at her kitchen table phone in hand and made mental notes as she listened to him. He was very distant on the phone and refused to provide her with a copy. After trying to approach her request in a number of ways she thought it might be better to see him face to face so she made an appointment with him for herself and Doc. It was clear to Stella that Jean had already spoken with the attorney. He treated Doc very poorly, as if she was stupid or unable to comprehend what he was saying, drawing circles on a piece of paper and saying, "These are your trusted people." Stella was flabbergasted. What was he doing? He was making an unsolicited mental assessment of Doc. Only after Stella became visibly upset did he review the trust and, since the trust identified

Stella as a trustee, agreed to have a copy made for her. What a slap in the face to Doc. She was seated in front of him and yet he ignored her. Stella remembered this attorney, as he was one who had advertised a free lunch for all people interested in estate planning. Doc and Stella attended the lunch and ended up having their estates placed into trust. Lesson learned, beware of a free lunch!

Stella and Doc left the attorney's office, but it was weeks before a copy of the trust arrived. She had questions about some of the legal jargon and called the trust attorney to ask him for clarification on language regarding the power of attorney and the trustee. He was vague and when Stella persisted, he advised her to engage another attorney. Well, thanks for nothing! She thought. She was convinced that he was not looking out for Doc's best interests and was possibly colluding with Jean. Stella then made a decision that would take her down an arduous road. For Doc's sake, she hoped she would prevail.

CHAPTER 6

Deception

In Doc's life, a pattern emerged from all of the craziness occurring around her. Jean and Beth told Doc, in both their words and deeds, that she was unable to make her own decisions. The strategy of demeaning and disrespecting her was not lost on Stella. Beth, in not assisting Doc with bathing or providing clean clothes, created a picture in which for the first time ever, Doc looked unkempt.

In June, Stella received an invitation to meet Jean and Beth at a local restaurant for dinner. She went, thinking that they wanted to set things straight and apologize for the terrible way they had treated her over Beth's daughters' previous complaint. That was not to be the case. Jean and Beth came separately with Beth arriving first. "Hello Beth" Stella greeted her as warmly as she could muster up". "Hello!" Awkward does not quite describe their interaction. Stella had no problem looking directly at Beth, but it was not reciprocated. Beth focused her attention on a potted plant in the corner waiting for Jean to arrive. It was almost comical and Stella began to enjoy just staring at Beth and watching her fix her mouth tightly to avoid speaking. Finally, Jean walked in looking like she hadn't slept in days and merely nodded when Stella greeted her.

After they were seated and ordered dinner Jean began to speak about the real reason for the dinner date. "Doc is deteriorating rapidly and it is becoming harder and harder to manage her." Stella sat quietly hoping against all hope that at some point in the rehearsed script she would actually speak the truth. It wasn't until she said, "We would like to have your schedule, and a commitment of days when you will be watching Doc and Aunt Rita." "Excuse me, what did you say?" Stella asked with just a touch of sarcasm added to her voice. She continued. "You have mistreated, maligned, disrespected me, accused me of mishandling Doc's money and now you want a schedule for when I will watch Doc and Rita?" Stella shook her head side to side and said, "No" to anyone listening.

Jean repeated her request as their entrees were brought to the table. Jean's words literally hung in the air as they all ate dinner in silence. Beth never looked up as she forked her steak and potatoes into her mouth and Stella had trouble swallowing so enraged that Jean had the audacity to once again discount her Aunt's wishes. The whole scene for anyone observing them must have been very perplexing.

Stella eventually raised her eyes to Jean and attempted to engage her to no avail. She moved on to look at Beth with her stare unwavering, not blinking but holding steadfast as she firmly told them off in a well-modulated voice, "I have been Doc's true and loyal friend and will always welcome her into my home and take her to the places that she enjoys, but under no circumstances will I become a caretaker to Doc and Rita. I am Doc's friend, not her caretaker and why would you expect me to be a caretaker since Beth, sitting here, is being paid to do that very thing, be a caretaker to Doc and Rita." In retrospect, her response was ingenious and in time would bode her well in her fight to help Doc. Jean was clasping and unclasping her hands, her anger was palpable and she nearly shouted when she replied. "Beth cannot possibly be expected to give total care to both Doc and Rita." Jean was trying desperately to keep her voice down but whatever was seething inside of her wanted to get out. "You know Jean, I look at this situation very differently and I wonder if you are taking into consideration what is expected of a caretaker and then compare that to what Beth actually fulfills." Stella responded fixing her gaze on Beth and seeing her squirm in her chair. "Beth is paid well; she enjoys free lodging and food for her and her family. Perhaps the problem lies in the fact that Beth has another commitment and works at the hospital two or three times a week. I would think the solution would be in securing another caretaker, part time, to fill in the days Beth is missing."

God that felt so good to be able to tell them to their face that she was not going to be stomped on and then told how best she could help them. The only one she planned on helping was Doc. That did it; Jean was exasperated, grabbed the bill and started to pay it. Stella's last response to her was simple as she placed forty dollars on the table and left. "I pay for my own dinner."

"Nothing is easier than to denounce the evildoer; nothing is more difficult than to understand him."
   Fyodor Dostoyevsky

Shortly after that dinner, Jean saw Stella working in her yard, approached her, and started to discuss an issue related to Doc's finances. "I have been looking for the title to Doc's car, I am unable to pay the car insurance without a clear title." Jean said. Stella nearly choked when she responded, "Really? I find that odd since Doc paid that bill and it is good for the next eight months and you don't need a title to renew insurance." Jean then changed her tact, saying, "We must clean these things up because the state will confiscate Doc's monies and properties upon her demise." There was no way for Stella to respond without getting into an altercation so she simply remained quiet as Jean turned and walked away. After this conversation, Stella consulted her attorney, describing Jean's request and concerns. He promptly responded to Jean with a copy to Stella, by letter, advising her to be cautious regarding the matter of car title and transfer of investments and to consult her attorney before proceeding.

Stella's mistrust of Jean continued to grow. In Doc's original living trust Jean was identified as power of attorney and Stella was named trustee. She studied her copy of the trust carefully to review her responsibilities as trustee.

As trustee, Stella was to see that Doc's wishes were followed as stipulated in the trust. Some of those wishes included, "I request that my disability trustee make every reasonable effort to see to it that I am taken care of in my own home or in the home of members of my family or loved ones and not placed in a long-term convalescent healthcare facility, nursing home, or any similar facility. In my own home, I find convenience, comfortable surroundings, and I can maintain my own privacy and my own dignity."

When Jean found and reviewed Doc's trust, she discovered that Doc had named her as the power of attorney. Originally Doc wanted to name Stella to be both power of attorney and trustee. Stella did not feel comfortable in being both. She advised Doc to name a family member as power of attorney, but agreed to be listed as trustee to ensure Doc's wishes were carried out. The trust specifically stated, "This right to amend or revoke my trust is personal to me and may not be exercised by any legal representative or agent acting on my behalf." When Jean discovered she was power of attorney she ignored this statement, and took it upon herself to amend the trust and remove Stella as the Trustee. This gave Jean exclusive control over the trust and Doc's finances. Henceforth, Stella had no input or knowledge or say so in the application of the trust.

As the storm gained momentum, that summer before Doc's incarceration, mistrust was a word on everyone's tongue. Jean and her crew tried in earnest to pull apart Doc's and Stella's friendship. Stella and her family had become a threat to them. While working in her yard, Stella often heard shouting coming from Doc's house. Beth was screaming at Doc and Doc was screaming back, 'This is my home and I can do what I want in my own home.' It took everything in Stella's power to keep silent and not interfere. She so wanted to walk over and have it out with Beth for showing such disdain and disrespect toward Doc but she worried that her interference would increase their mistreatment of her friend.

Summer had always been a pleasant time for Doc and Stella. Their yards seemed as one as there was nothing to interrupt the flow of soft green grass between the houses. Stella could stand on her deck and look across to see Doc's patio. Their days often began with sitting on Stella's deck, sipping coffee and reading the newspaper. The yard had become her daughter Anne's canvas as she spent her free days away from the university classroom strategically placing plants where their beauty could be most admired. She oversaw the flower beds, inserting Art Deco and shimmering stones to enhance the visual feast. Anne even built a grotto with a statue of the Blessed Mother for Doc. Anne spent entire days potting herbs and vegetables and Doc drank it all in, sitting on the deck, reading and praying, while birds chirped and tree branches swayed in the cool summer morning.

Anne and Stella engaged Doc in conversations, to keep her abreast of the news, but more so to gauge her ability to recall events and people, to assess the stages of her memory loss. Early on in her disease, she could recall events and people with little problem, but eventually it became obvious that her memory was waning. Stella, however, was never convinced that Doc's symptoms were strictly due to the assumed Alzheimer's disease. Doc had also been diagnosed with a benign pseudo tumor behind her left eye that was growing insidiously every day. Stella questioned whether the pressure from this tumor might also mimic a decrease in ability to recall events and people. Whereas most Alzheimer's patients have a flat or non-responsive affect, Doc, when recalling bits of memory, showed all the appropriate facial expressions to mirror what she recalled. She wasn't a typical Alzheimer patient.

As the summer progressed an old friend of Doc's made the trip from California to visit her. Jackie and Doc had been friends for a very long time and had traveled on vacations across the country together. She was a short, stocky lady with out of control gray hair and bushy eyebrows to match. Large blue sparkly eyes peeked out from under a baseball cap that sat perched on her head. Over the years she and Doc had remained close friends in spite of the distance between them. Upon arrival it didn't take long for Jackie to pick up on the tension in Doc's house. Negativity and unhappiness hung in the air like a putrid stench. She preferred visiting with Doc in Stella's home, which was a blessing for Stella as she could see two old friends happy to be with one another. After a day of visiting, Jackie approached Stella and said, "What the heck is going on over there" tilting her head toward Doc's house. Acknowledging the situation, Stella responded, "It's been a living hell for Doc. I've made it a point to bring her here as often as possible Jackie, because honestly, I'm afraid I'll make it worse for her if I am in her house with Beth and the others. They all seem so intent on proving to Doc that she's slipping and not remembering and doing things that frankly are just lies. "What about Rita, how do they treat her?" inquired Jackie. "Because she doesn't rely on them for much, they literally leave her alone to do her own thing." Stella responded, adding, "Neither Doc nor Rita have any power in that house, its pitiful to see and hear the disrespect floating around there."

That evening Jackie and Stella spoke at length about Doc's situation with Jackie saying " They treat her like a child telling her what she can and can't do, where she can go, what clothes to put on, and what to eat. From what I've observed it's all meant to demean her and take away her identity. Frankly I don't know how she stands it. She was always such an independent person."

During one of Doc and Jackie's visit, Doc said, "Jean won't give me any of my own money." She didn't look at them but down at her hands as if she was ashamed for some unknown reason. Jackie was so upset with that particular revelation that she jumped at the opportunity when she was alone with Jean to say, "Jean, Doc has confided in me that you won't give her any of her own money. Is there a problem with letting her have money?" Jackie could be very direct when needed and put people in their place if need be. "She just gives it all away. When we went to church she gave the priest a hundred dollars. I mean, she has no concept whatsoever of the value of money. I'm just protecting her interest." Jackie wasn't buying Jean's reasoning because even with the changes in her friend's life she knew that Doc was fully cognizant of the value of money.

Later at Stella's house she relayed what Jean said about Doc and money. "Okay, according to Jean, Doc has been loose with her money and gives it away willy-nilly even giving the priest at church a hundred-dollar bill". Stella clarified by saying, "That is not true Jackie, I know because Doc told me that Jean would not give her any money to keep in her wallet saying you don't need any money." I know how important it is to Doc to have money in her wallet and I gave her a hundred-dollar bill in addition to four five-dollar bills. That was a month ago and last week I asked if she still had the money. She showed me her wallet and there was still a hundred plus one five-dollar bill. Doc said she never leaves her wallet for anyone to see and that she even sleeps with it for fear they would take it from her. After mass Doc usually gives the priest five bucks and tells him to buy a coke. She really likes him and often after his homily will shout that he did "a good job." "Ha! I can just see her doing that. You know Stella, I never saw Doc pass by anyone with his or her hand out without putting something into his or her palm. They would be standing with their cardboard sign and everyone whizzing past and Doc would make it a point to stop and talk with them, encourage them and give them a little something." I know what you mean Jackie. Once I asked her if she thought any of them were frauds and she said." 'Who are we to judge?' I guess that sums her up well.

The following day Jackie began the long trip home, but this time with a heavy heart and a promise to return as quickly as possible.

I had to give it to Jean who was dauntless in her effort to

weave so called evidence into proof that Doc had lost her mind. The latest lie was spewed out in October when Stella asked Jean what happened to Doc's cell phone, "I've disconnected Doc's cell phone as she has incurred a bill of over six hundred dollars calling infomercials." That just did not sound like something that Doc would be interested in doing so, Stella investigated through the phone provider and found that Doc never exceeded her monthly plan of forty dollars and that there never was a call to any infomercial.

Not wanting to get into an argument with Jean, she wrote a letter and gave it to her after mass the following Sunday, detailing what she had learned from the phone company. Stella also informed her that because of Jean's concern over the phone bill, she had purchased a phone for Doc and would pay for it herself.

Jean had discovered yet another way to keep Stella and Doc apart. Though Jean was not a churchgoer, she had begun to take her aunts to church every week and thus deny Stella the pleasure of praying with her friend. In church, Stella would position herself in the pew behind Doc and give her back a little push to let her know she was there. Doc was always happy to see her, and Stella would quickly maneuver a way to walk her out of the church knowing that Jean could not make a scene right there with parishioners around. Doc would invite her to join them for brunch with Stella responding, "Jean would not like that". "Who cares, I'm the one paying, as Jean uses my credit card."

It took a few days for Jean to respond to Stella regarding her letter. She phoned Stella screaming, "You are encroaching upon my authority over my Aunt. I will not tolerate this and will seek legal action if I must." Stella was beyond being afraid of Jean and said in a quiet tone, "You do whatever you think you need to do." The only response she got was the disconnect tone buzzing in her ear.

While Stella traveled to Savannah for a short vacation, Jean took advantage of her absence and further isolated her from Doc by disconnecting the house phone in Docs bedroom. Days passed and a terrible worry hung over Stella's head. She could not reach Doc and when she called Rita's phone, someone would intercept the call and hang up. Stella was frantic, worried that Doc had fallen or was incapacitated in some way. After her many attempts to call doc and Rita's phones, she contacted Nancy, a friend of Doc's, and pleaded with her to intervene and call Rita. It took Nancy two days to reach Rita, but when she did she also asked to speak with Doc and then called Stella with the news that Doc was okay. Her prayers were answered. Doc told Nancy that, according to Jean, her phones were not working. Upon Stella's return she was still unable to contact Doc. Not having the ability to visit or even talk on the phone with her, Stella continued to worry daily about how Doc must feel.

Every day brought more drama. One day while in her yard, Stella saw Jean and asked, "Is Doc able to use the cell phone I've purchased for her?" If looks could kill, Stella would be dead. Jean responded, "I have no knowledge of any phone, I don't know what you are talking about." A heated exchange ensued. Stella thought, I'm already in trouble with this crazy woman I might as well go all the way and said, "You know Jean I took a number of my paintings and loaned them to Doc for the house. I marked the backs with my name and address. Are they still hanging in the living and dining rooms?" Once again Stella got the same exasperated response from Jean as she abruptly turned her back and walked away. "Well, that was a revelation," thought Stella. For all intent and purposes, turmoil was the flavor of the day in Doc's world.

The situation weighed heavily upon Doc. Each time she came over to Stella's it took her longer and longer to shrug off what was happening. On top of everything else, Doc was experiencing more pain in her left eye as the tumor was growing. One day, Jean approached Anne while she was weeding flower beds in the yard, "Anne, I need you and your mother's support to encourage Doc to return to the eye specialist for surgery. Doc is refusing to go." "What makes you think that she will go if my mother asks?" responded Anne. "Doc always says she will only go if your mother takes her." Anne could hear the thread of disgust in Jean's voice for having to ask Stella for any favor. Anne cut off the conversation saying, "I'll let my mom know," and returned to her weeding.

The next time Doc walked over to Stella's, they were enjoying a cup of coffee on the deck and Stella took the opportunity to say, "Doc, I can see from the way you are shielding your eye that the tumor is causing you more pain. Please as a favor to me, agree to have the eye surgery. It will make everything less painful for you." "If you come with me, I'll go Stella." "Good!" Stella was relieved but something continued to gnaw at her, and she didn't quite believe that all would go as planned.

Days before her appointment, Doc attended bingo with Beth. On the way home, she called Stella from Beth's phone. Stella could hear her asking Beth what time her surgery was scheduled. Beth said she didn't know. On the eve of the appointment, Stella walked Doc home after a visit. Jean came to the door and said, "You are not allowed to accompany Doc to her appointment because you are not her caretaker." She said almost gleefully. "I'm not going as her caretaker but as her friend." Stella reminded her. Jean grew agitated and began issuing other orders regarding Doc and Stella's time together. She ended by saying, "In the future you must have Doc use the ramp in the garage instead of the front stairs, because she's previously fallen on the stairs." This was unbelievable Stella thought. I was the one who found Doc on the steps when she broke her hip. Stella could not resist looking at Jean and stating, "I always accompany Doc home and help her into the house. I suggest you do the same when she comes unannounced and unaccompanied to my house. As for the eye surgery, you need to tell Doc that there has been a change in plans as it was Doc who asked me to go in the first place." For the past thirty years as her friend, Stella accompanied her for all her surgeries, which included repair of a rotary cuff of her shoulder, two eye surgeries for reduction of the tumor, hernia repair, two knee replacements, and a surgery on her arm. Is it any wonder that Doc only trusted Stella?

Later, Doc called Stella and said that Beth would be driving them in the morning. Not knowing the exact time, Stella arose early the next day and was dressed and ready to go. She was not convinced that they would allow her to go with Doc. She saw Beth and Beverly, Jean's daughter, get in the car with Doc and leave from the top of their driveway. They started down the circular drive toward Stella's home and then suddenly turned the car in the opposite direction. When Doc realized what was happening, she opened her car door, forcing Beth to stop. She jumped out of the car and stood in the middle of the street yelling, "Shit on a stick!" Beth was yelling as well, "Get back in the car, are you crazy? You could have hurt yourself." Stella couldn't remember ever hearing Doc swear! It was a testament to Doc's intelligence that even with pressure in her brain from the tumor, she clearly understood the subterfuge going on around her. Doc walked as quickly as she could to Stella's driveway and up toward the front door. She was extremely distraught. Stella helped her into the house while Beth shrieked, "This is all your fault." Stella could not hold her tongue. With the front door open she no longer cared if neighbors heard or not and said loud and clear, "What you are doing? Your treatment of my friend is tantamount to abuse and you should all burn in Hell."

Doc remained at Stella's home for the better part of the day seemingly reluctant to return home. In the evening Stella's sister Marie came over to visit, "Doc you seem upset, what has happened?" "I was supposed to go to the eye doctor and Stella was coming with me, but my keeper tried to pull a fast one on me and didn't pick up Stella, so I jumped out of the car. She wasn't very happy." Throughout the evening Doc asked Marie repeatedly if it was safe to go home. Stella felt that Doc was afraid that there would be repercussions stemming from her refusal to keep the appointment. Poor Doc, now she was even afraid to go into her own home. After Doc was walked home and safely inside, Stella said to her daughter Anne, "There is a bully in that house and it's Beth."

It always amazed Stella how Jean's plan to discredit her and break apart their friendship had multiple twists and turns. For instance, on one of the infrequent times that Stella was inside Doc's home, she noticed that the many-framed pictures of herself, her family and Doc were now missing from her bedroom. She casually said to Doc, "Your room looks so clean, but what has happened to our pictures that used to be on top of the bookcase?"

Beth who had been eavesdropping outside Doc's bedroom, rushed in, screaming at the top of her lungs like a crazy lady, "Doc has Alzheimer's and all you do is upset her. You're a horrible person." Stella responded to her in a modulated tone. "You know Beth, you seem to have a problem in getting along with people. You need help." "I need help? You're the only person I have any trouble with." "Well, that's not entirely true, I know about the fight with Rita." Stella had recalled a conversation with Doc from the previous week in which Doc said that Beth and Rita had a terrible fight and Beth packed up and left, adding, "Thank God." Beth couldn't handle any more and responded saying, "Out, get out of here." Stella, not backing down, responded, "This is Doc's home and only she can order me to leave." It's funny how people's true colors come out during arguments. Beth dialed Jean's number, spoke to her and handed the phone to Stella. Jean ordered her from the house, threatening to have Stella arrested and escorted out by police. Stella knew that, without guardianship, Jean had no authority to prohibit visits. She said, "I suppose when you obtain guardianship you will restrain me from visiting Doc?" "You are darned right!" and hung up. At last the truth was out.

Before Christmas, Jean made an appointment at the gerontologist for Doc. One morning Stella picked up Doc and they treated themselves to a breakfast of waffles. Doc told Stella about the visit but couldn't elaborate on why she had to go there. Her family physician, Dr. Pilano, had received the gerontologist's report of Doc's testing and was monitoring the treatment. It seemed so strange that Jean insisted on taking Doc back to the gerontologist. "I don't know why she took me there." Doc said. Her eyebrows were drawn together and she looked very puzzled." It was probably just a routine visit." Responded Stella. "I don't think so, since I just saw Dr. Pilano for my medication." Doc was looking off into space and then verbalized her worst fear. "Stella, I'm afraid that she will put me in a mental institution." Stella was instantly suspicious, she didn't trust Jean and wondered if the appointment was a ruse by Jean to ingratiate herself with the gerontologist. In that type of medical setting she could talk doctor to doctor and assess whether anything had been documented that would indicate that Doc was not of sound mind. That certainly would be useful to Jean if she was attempting to discredit the trust, since Doc would have been incompetent at the time of its last review.

Tears were always a breath away during that time. Thinking back, it's a wonder that Stella didn't become dehydrated from crying. Tears do release stress but they also blur what is actually taking place. Every day, she awoke with a singular purpose to do less crying and more praying. She was intent on being proactive, not sitting idly by while her friend was being waked and buried before her eyes.

CHAPTER 7

Isolation

The months between Christmas and Easter were difficult to endure as Doc was being systematically removed from having contact with Stella. In search of any opportunity to be able to see her friend, Stella would look out the window to see if Beth or Jean might take Doc to Tuesday night bingo. One Tuesday, when she saw the car leave the driveway, Stella waited ten minutes and proceeded to the bingo hall. When she arrived, Doc was seated alone, looking disheveled and forlorn. Her face lit up when she saw Stella. Motioning her with her hands she said, "Hurry before Jean sees you and makes me go home." Stella turned and saw Jean buying bingo cards and calculated that she had at least five minutes to talk with her friend. Her heart broke when Doc said, "So this is how it all ends. After working my whole life, I have nothing." The women nearby knew Stella as she used to bring Doc to bingo before Doc's family became involved. Hurriedly, they asked Stella "What in the hell is going on? We don't like the way Beth interacts with Doc when she brings her." They said that when Doc won the one thousand dollar coverall, Beth would not let them give her the money. Doc interrupted saying, "I think Beth kept the money for herself." When Jean returned and saw Stella, she was taken aback glaring at her with contempt, but unable to act on that since they were in a very public space. When the bingo games commenced, Stella gave Doc a big hug saying, "I love you Doc see you soon."

"I believe we are free within limits, and yet there is an unseen hand, a guiding angel, that somehow, like a submerged propeller, drives us on."

Rabindranath Tagore

A few weeks later on Valentine's Day, Stella and Anne walked over to Doc's with a few small gifts and cards and a special poem penned by Stella about friendship. Beverly, Jean's daughter, greeted them at the door, "I'm sorry but I'm not allowed to let you in." Beverly seemed sincere when she said this and with no animosity. Doc must have heard them talking and came out of her room. Stella brushed past Beverly and handed the gifts and cards to Doc. saying, "I'm going to be gone for a few weeks to Savannah, I'll be thinking of you Doc. I'll phone you so we can talk every day. I hope you enjoy my special note one friend to another." "I wish I could go with you Stella, have a good time," said Doc. As Stella and her daughter were walking down the front steps, Jean pulled into the driveway, rolled down the window and yelled, "Get off this property. I am having an order of protection invoked so that you can never come here again". Her eyes were glaring and she spoke with such malice that her cheek twitched from holding her lips tightly across her teeth. Stella stood her ground and said, "You have no authority yet to stop me from coming onto Doc's property." Stella was well aware that only Doc could do that. My God, Jean was like a crazy lady thought Stella. Safely inside her own home Stella watched as Jean stormed up Doc's steps and slammed the front door.

Each day from that point forward, life for Doc was anything but peaceful. Stella knew her friend well and could only imagine the argument that she put forward to the strangers in her home regarding whether she could visit with Stella or not. She was adamant against being told how her life was to be lived. During this period, Stella underwent a medical evaluation at the hospital. During the test her thoughts wandered and she focused on Jean and her threat of a 'protective order,' praying with all her heart to God and Doc's recently departed priest friend, Father John, to please allow her to see her friend again. It had been almost a month since Jean threatened her with a protective order and Stella was worried every day about Doc being isolated. Apparently, God and Father John heard her prayer. Upon leaving the hospital Doc called and told Stella in an excited voice, "I'm coming over to visit." "That will be fine Doc, but I won't be home for another thirty minutes. I'm just now leaving the hospital."

Stella was hopeful that Doc was coming over, but in the past, she would receive a follow up call from Doc saying that she wasn't allowed to come. She had planned on doing some shopping and was going to proceed but thought it was best to go home just in case a visit actually materialized. The ride home from the hospital took about twenty-five minutes and much to her surprise when she arrived, standing at her front door was Doc accompanied by her nephew Phil. Going forward, Doc once more began to walk across the grass to Stella's house on an almost daily basis. The only time she seemed relaxed was when Anne and Stella fixed her favorite foods and made her laugh. During those short visits, life seemed calm and normal. Stella had become aware of a recent flurry of activity at Doc's house, new appliances, including a refrigerator, washer, dryer, and dishwasher were delivered, and cars would come and go, mostly at night. As she watched this activity she couldn't help but think that Jean was now allowing Doc to visit so that she would be out of the way and Jean could carry out her plan.

On June nineteenth, Stella had not heard from Doc for two days and was beginning to worry. She had a sick feeling in her gut and knew something was very wrong. Stella had traveled to her son's home getting ready to babysit her grandchildren when Doc called her. Before she could ask her where she was, a nurse quickly intercepted the call. The reality of what the nurse said, coupled with the total terror she heard in her friend's voice brought tears to her eyes. She asked to speak with Doc and heard her say that she was in prison and please come help her. To Stella, Doc's plea sounded like a screech from a wounded animal gasping its last breath. Panic gripped Stella. She told Doc she would be there as soon as possible, grabbed her car keys, and told her son that she needed to leave.

A river of tears began to flow that day.

CHAPTER 8

Legal Pursuit

Stella's world took a dramatic shift and launched into an unthinkable darkness. There were no more moments of Doc seated on Stella's back deck enjoying the sheer beauty of God's nature, breathing in the fresh air and listening to the sounds of the woods. In its place was an alternative existence in which Doc dwelled and in her words everyone is pathetic and she would likely join them if she remained there. Her words haunted Stella. Stella was deeply concerned about her once independently, free friend. A resolve to be more than just a friend to Doc emerged as Stella realized how quickly isolation and captivity would deplete even a strong person's will to live. She believed that in order to save Doc, she would have to become a lifeline for her. She committed to being there for her every day to keep her talking and thinking and in contact with the world. She didn't know how to unravel the web that Jean had spun to entrap Doc but she did believe that everything started with the first step, so she began investigating the legal avenues available to her to get Doc out of the locked Alzheimer's unit and back into her own home.

"To truly strip a man of everything, one must take away his money, community, and the core of his beliefs until he is bathed in the agony of isolation."
    Leinad Eibam

Stella was scheduled to fly to Savannah in a week. She went to see Doc to let her know that she would be gone for two weeks. Doc was in her room with the television on watching one of the game shows. She looked so frail and sad sitting there. Committed to boosting her spirit Stella put a wide smile on her face and greeted her dear friend. "Hi Doc." Stella was on a mission and had Doc up and walking with her down to the park area where they sat and listened to wonderful music. Finally, Stella approached the subject saying, "I'm taking a short trip to Savannah and should be back in two weeks. I will be here the minute I get back and I promise to bring you your favorites." "Ice Cream and Waffles?" asked Doc with an impish smile. "Absolutely!" Doc sat pensively in her chair and Stella made small talk about calling her every day and reassured her that Anne would visit. Doc looked up with her straight forward gaze and said, "The one person in my family that I have trusted is evil and has shattered and broken my trust. I am in prison, Stella, the worst place I could ever be. I don't know if I can survive being locked up." Stella reeled and looked for something to hold on to. Her world had spun out of control. Her friend was in a bottomless pit. All she could do was cry.

From the beginning of Doc's incarceration, Stella placed a calendar on the small bulletin board in Doc's room. Each month, she would post a new page so she could scratch out the dates, one by one. Before Stella traveled, she put a smiley face on the date of her return to alleviate any fears Doc might have about her absence. In addition, she left a stash of Hershey bars, Doc's favorite, with the nursing staff to give Doc as surprise treats, especially if she was feeling blue.

Stella kept her promise and saw Doc the morning after she

returned from Savannah. Doc gave her a big smile and clearly seemed excited to see her or maybe it was the ice cream and waffles. As they sat in her room and talked, Doc expressed "I am so angry Stella I can't cry. I feel like I could erupt just like a volcano." Stella could sense the terror that Doc was experiencing. The person that she thought would always have her back had turned on her. Her freedom was gone. There were strangers all around her. Stella felt a tiny twinge of relief that at least Doc was able to express some of the feelings she was experiencing, perhaps enough so that the volcanic eruption would be held at bay.

Upon leaving the nursing home one day, Stella walked by an office of the ombudsman who is hired by the hospital to advocate for patients. She saw a man sitting behind the desk, but instead of approaching him then she made a mental note to call from home and discuss whether Doc's family had a legal right to stop her from seeing Doc. Having been told by Jean that she could not take Doc off the unit, Stella suspected that Jean would try to prohibit her from visiting as well. When she arrived home, Stella called the ombudsman's office. "I am interested in knowing if my friend's niece, her guardian, can bar me from visiting her? Do I have any recourse if that occurs?" Looking back, Stella was shocked, not so much by his words, but by his curt tone. "If the guardian restricts you, you have no recourse," was the Ombudsman's response. He said this with such a haughty tone that Stella was now convinced that Jean, who had been on the staff of the hospital affiliated with the nursing home, had already spoken with him and laid the groundwork to stop her visits with Doc.

It is difficult to put into words what Doc's daily life entailed. Envision waking up in your own space, seeing your own bedroom, hearing your own sounds, but the first peek as you lift your eyelids is not home but a cold, strange environment. How do you summon the courage to live another day? The people Doc took her meals with were, God help them, nearly out of touch with reality. Doc thirsted for real conversation, for any semblance of normalcy, but what she saw and heard was twisted and abnormal. Stella believed that in order to survive, Doc withdrew into her room because she could put on the television, hear normal conversation and understand what was going on in the world.

The staff told Stella that Doc liked to engage with them, talk and joke about everyday things. Stella had a conversation with the housekeeper, who asked, "Why is Doc here?" "Well, her family thought that she needed to be here." A frown crossed the housekeeper's forehead as she said," I am always happy cleaning her room because we talk and she's even encouraging me to go to school so that I can get a better job. I just love her."

The staff was good to Doc, always suggesting that she join in activities and being part of groups but being around the other residents only made her feel worse. During a discussion with the staff, Stella said, "I notice that you all address Doc as Mary. You know she is a physician, right? All of her friends and patients only refer to her as Doc." The staff nurses told Stella that Jean never mentioned the fact that Doc was a physician. From that time forward, she was referred to as Doc. With the staff encouragement, she attempted to play bingo but the patients continually asked what number was called, not once but twenty times. They shouted "Bingo!" after only two numbers. To add insult to injury, when Doc won, they paid her with play money, which they called funny money.

Doc's intelligence fought against slipping away into oblivion. There were times when she could feel herself losing ground and she lashed out. Stella felt that her daily visits helped to keep those moments to a minimum. She wasn't sure if Doc's behavior might have escalated but she never wanted to take the chance. Some visits were quiet, with Stella seated on the bed and Doc watching television or dozing in her chair with her favorite classical music playing in the background. Other visits were filled with getting Doc into the shower, washing her hair, and making sure that she had clean clothes to wear.

The reality of what Doc had become stared back at her in every mirror. The Doc she now viewed in drab colored gym clothes was a stark contrast to the Doc in starched, brightly colored cotton blouses and crisp pants. During visits, Doc would often be quiet and respond with single words to any inquiry, but at the end of Stella and Doc's time together, she would grow animated, talkative, and interactive. Stella continued to struggle with trying to find the words to explain why Jean had institutionalized her friend. When Doc asked why she was in a locked unit, she usually answered, "You need to ask Jean that." It took Stella a long time to finally answer with the truth.

CHAPTER 9

Lis Pendens

As Doc was no longer in her home, Beth and her family had left as well. Jean began to disassemble Doc's home, cleaned out Doc's garage, and gave away or sold furniture and other household items. One of her nephews appeared out of the blue and was seen painting the entrance way into the house. Stella suspected that Jean was getting ready to sell the house so she contacted her attorney and asked him what recourse she would have if the house was being sold. He advised Stella to notify him when a "For Sale" sign appeared in the yard. Within two weeks Stella received a call from her daughter while she was with Doc, "Mom, I just saw a For Sale sign on Doc's front lawn."

"Tricks and treachery are the practice of fools that don't have brains enough to be honest."
Benjamin Franklin

Let the games begin! For too long, Stella had felt powerless. But with Jean's audacity in placing Doc's home up for sale, a burst of hope enveloped her. Doc's house was held in trust and thus was not available for sale. In a hurry to sell, Jean had listed the home for fifty percent below market value. According to the real estate agent, a cash offer had already been accepted. Upon Stella's request, her attorney sent a certified letter to the realtor agent, advising that the house was held in trust with a pending lawsuit and thus was not able to be sold. How Stella wished she could have been a fly on the wall to see Jean's response to the news that the sale could not proceed. But Stella knew Jean well and expected that repercussions were sure to follow. Stella's attorney, with whom she was in frequent contact, gave her some unsolicited advice. "Stella, I charge a well deserved but hefty fee and I'm concerned that the case could drag on for months and months and that could become very costly. I think you would do just as well with a local attorney who doesn't have the same fee based services as I do." He gave Stella the name of one whom he trusted. His name was Vic Marshall and Stella made an appointment for the next day.

After the meeting, Stella found it difficult to describe Vic. He was an unassuming man, not a high-profile legal eagle, but in his questions and explanations he made her feel that his grasp of the law was firm. Stella inquired, "Do you think I have any legal standing in filing a petition to get my friend out of the Alzheimer Unit?" Stella crossed her fingers and held her breath. "I believe there may be a slim chance that we will prevail. The first step will be to reestablish you as the designated disability trustee as stated in your friend's trust. This is the beginning of many legal hurdles to come, but a necessary one." When Vic and Stella met again in two days she solidified the agreement by submitting a retainer. Then, Vic advised her, "I will immediately file a Lis pendens in court. That should prohibit the sale of Doc's home, as it is a written notice to all parties that a lawsuit has been filed concerning the property," and as an after thought, Vic said, " I'll also file for a court hearing to designate you as the disability trustee." After filing the Lis pendens, the sale of the house was stopped. Additionally, Vic said, "You may possibly obtain Doc's release from the Alzheimer unit if we, through questioning Jean's actions prove that they were contrary to Doc's stated wishes."

My God, could it be true? Could she actually, with the help of this quiet, thoughtful attorney, see Doc released? Her heart raced. This was the first time in this ordeal that she felt any glimmer of hope. Walking out of his office, Stella began to call everyone who knew of the situation and ask them to pray that they would be successful.

Prayer could sometimes be a mystery to Stella but never to Doc. She had always been the instrument of the most high and had been rewarded with the ability to pray in simple, unfettered ways. Stella remembered driving with her up into the mountains near Savannah on one of their trips. She was like a child with her eyes lifted to the top of the mountains. Her prayer was a simple "Thank you God that I have eyes to see." Stella wondered if Doc could pray on that unit. There doesn't seem to be any quiet time for prayer, what with the patients in different stages of Alzheimer's walking the hallways day and night, talking and mumbling. Stella saw the tremendous strain placed upon Doc from having to interact with the patients. It was unnerving to her to have the other patients walk into her room unannounced. In those instances, she became very agitated and so, true to that intelligent mind of hers, she devised a plan to thwart the wayward patients. Her solution was simple: she placed a tall, artificial potted tree just in front of her door and affixed a large, red stop sign to the door above a handwritten sign that read "DO NOT ENTER." Where on earth did she get that tree? And does anyone really believe an Alzheimer's patient has the ability to create solutions like that? Clearly, Doc did not belong there.

Stella implemented her own creative plan. Even though she

was fearful of repercussions from Jean, Stella took every opportunity to bring Doc into a sane environment. The symphony was scheduled to perform on the grounds of the nursing home and though Jean had prohibited Stella from taking Doc off the unit, Stella informed the nursing staff and took Doc outside to enjoy the music. The next day, the cleaning lady told Stella of a conversation she overheard between Doc and her sister Rita. "I enjoyed the symphony last evening. The music was so beautiful." As if she were a child, Jean, who had brought Rita for a visit, corrected Doc, saying, "You heard the music through the window." Doc turned, looked Jean squarely in the face, and said, "No, Stella came and took me to the concert." Stella wasn't sure if Doc was cognizant of the power that Jean held over her, but occasionally, the old Doc came through. Stella was quite sure that Jean recognized this version of Doc and, like a snake, scurried off to her hole in the ground.

The fall arrived and a pleasant nurse on the unit informed Stella and Doc that there was a beautiful garden next to the main dining room on the first floor and she saw no reason why Stella couldn't take Doc there since it was within the nursing home complex. It had a waterfall and statues of St. Francis of Assisi and the Blessed Mother. Doc had a deep devotion to Mary, the Mother of God, and in the garden, she would speak to her saying, "Sweet Mother help me in my time of sorrow. Please help me to get out of here." The tree in the center was bursting with fall colors, bright orange and muted reds with specks of yellow. Doc was in heaven. She laughed and talked about all sorts of things, it was as if they were back home and she was free.

Once again, Stella was struck by the cruelty of what had happened and would forever want to know why. Why would a niece, a physician in her own right, subject the person who showered her with gifts, strip her aunt's remaining coherent years of joy? Had Jean suffered some sort of nervous breakdown? Did the loss of her husband harden her? How did she have the nerve to walk on the unit knowing that the nurses who cared for Doc were very aware that Doc did not belong there? Stella was tortured, trying to understand Jean's motives and unable to understand, she was even more unable to forgive.

Just when Stella began to come to terms with what had happened to Doc, a new piece of information came to light. During the discovery phase of her lawsuit, copies of letters from two physicians detailing Doc's physical and mental status were discovered. The reports diagnosed her as incapacitated and unable to make financial decisions. One of the physicians, a radiation oncologist upon Jean's recommendation, saw Doc in Stella's presence for a brief fifteen minute consultation for the tumor growth behind her left eye. Three months later, he submitted a letter to the courts that Doc was "not able to be responsible for her financial affairs due to her dementia and confusion." The second physician was mentored by Doc and cared for her with love and attention. Her recommendation also identified her progressing post-stroke dementia and suggested that she was unable to make medical and financial decisions. Neither physician stated that she could not be cared for in her own home nor did they recommend admission to a locked Alzheimer's unit.

Almost every day, Doc would ask, "When can I go home?" Stella struggled with being totally honest with Doc and telling her everything about her legal pursuit, or just notifying her if and when her returning home was a possibility. What if it all fell through? How devastating that would be for Doc. Stella decided to simply inform Doc that she had hired a lawyer to assist in getting Doc returned back to her own home. She said, "I'm praying Doc, please pray for my special intention." Doc then asked, "What happened to my house and my money?" Stella reassured her that everything was still there. She didn't have the heart to tell her that she had observed Jean's crew removing furniture from the house and she assumed that if they were doing that they probably took her jewelry and other personal possessions. Stella would simply say, "Don't worry Doc, leave the worrying to me since nobody does it better than me." Doc would smile and chuckle. They sat in silence sometimes, lost in their own thoughts, and Stella was continually amazed at the trust between them. She trusted Doc with her life and Doc trusted Stella to help her get home. Stella felt an enormous weight upon her shoulders.

Stella observed that humans, when at their wit's ends, do their best to create sane environments regardless of the insanity engulfing them, so, Stella planned a picnic with two of her good friends for Doc to enjoy. "We're going to have the best time Doc; our friends are coming and we can use the room off the park to set up our picnic basket." The basket was filled with food and a bottle of wine and one of grape spritzer. What fun they had, laughing, engaging Doc in conversation, and watching her sit at the piano and play songs from memory. The day brought tears to everyone's eyes. That wonderful lady was not about to allow a premature and wrongful admission dictate how her brain functioned. During this and other visits they often sang songs together with Doc. One time when it was just Stella and Doc, Stella recorded Doc singing "My Buddy" on her cell phone.

Whenever Stella felt alone or especially vulnerable, she replayed this simple tune. Hearing her friend's voice gave her encouragement.

With a few exceptions, Stella visited Doc every day, usually for three hours, and found that she enjoyed the late afternoon and early evening visits best. Stella helped Doc shower, put on clean pajamas, and brush her beautiful natural teeth. Then Stella would watch her visibly relax awaiting sleep. Simple loving deeds, one friend to another.

CHAPTER 10

Trustee Designation

Doc's friend, Jackie, visited her once again having driven three days across the country by herself. Stella felt empathy for these two friends but more so for Doc when she imagined how ghastly it must have been to have to greet her old and dear friend in a locked Alzheimer's unit. During their first visit Doc was quiet, embarrassed that her friend was seeing her under such circumstances. Somewhere in that discomfort Doc realized how truly blessed she was to have strong and true friendships in her life. Stella was pleased that Doc was more herself and conversed with Jackie at length during their second visit. Later, around six p.m. Jean brought Rita for a visit with her sister. There was always frost in the air when Jean was around so Stella excused herself, telling Doc she'd be down the hall and left and allowed Jackie to remain and talk with Jean about Doc.

Later, at Stella's home, Jackie and Stella were relaxing on the deck and Jackie said, "Jean is mad about the lawsuit you filed, she thinks it's just a ploy to get Doc's house." Stella shook her head, "Jackie, I don't give a damn what Jean thinks, I am fighting to return Doc to her home". Stella thought, ' How long do I have to put up with the personal affronts coming from this evil woman?' and said out loud, "I should sue her for defamation of character." Shaking her head as she threw out any further thoughts about suing Jean, Stella realized that her biggest difficulty involved forgiveness. She didn't want to feel animosity towards Jean but as more lies were revealed any chance of forgiving her was thrown out the window. The following day Jackie visited Doc for the final time before beginning her return trip home. Stella had the sense that Jackie was fearful that this might have been the last time she saw her old friend.

> *"Friends share an interior space of a greater dimension"*
> **Anonymous**

In November, Stella had been informed that a court appointed guardian would visit Doc to ascertain her ability to be cared for in her home. Stella was eager to share the news with Doc but also a little worried about what her reaction might be. "Doc, a court appointed guardian will be coming to visit you. It's important that you answer all of her questions. I really think this is an encouraging sign. This person's only job is to represent you and report to the court."

Stella looked within herself and thought about her worst fear, that Doc would remain institutionalized and have to live out her days sequestered from her friend. Would God be so cruel as to allow that? She continued to struggle with her faith. She put herself in the category of those who believe ninety percent of the time but questions the other ten. Not so with Doc, who always said, "Put your problems in the hands of the Lord and pray to Saint Jude, the patron saint of hopeless cases." Stella wondered if, at the beginning of each life God assigns a person to come into our lives and keep us on the right track? If he does, surely Doc was assigned to help her.

The first court date was set for the end of November. On that day, both Doc and Jean's lawyers went to court and the case was postponed until after Christmas, at which time a decision would be made by the judge regarding Doc's ability to be cared for and remain in her own home. From everything that Vic shared with Stella, she knew that the proceeding was complicated and that the court moves at its own pace. Having Doc's future placed in the hands of strangers was very difficult for Stella. First, the judge had to review reports from everyone concerned, and then consider the trust that was filed regarding Doc's wishes. The lawsuit would not have progressed to this point except for one passage in the trust that stated, "This right to amend or revoke my trust is personal to me and may not be exercised by any legal representative or agent acting on my behalf." In other words, Doc's trust, which clearly outlined her wishes to remain in her home with help if need be could not nor should not be broken nor amended, even after declaration of incompetence and the emergence of the power of attorney.

Days stumbled along with daily visits to Doc in the morning, noon, or night. Some days were so filled with music and laughter that it seemed like the walls of the Alzheimer's unit disappeared and they were once again at home, sitting around the table with their coffee and doughnuts. Other days, the demons appeared, and sadness and depression was at their doorstep and they had to battle them again and replace despair with hope.

Christmas was just around the corner and Stella's children had purchased a Christmas tree with lights and ornaments, and a nightlight fashioned to look like the nativity scene for Doc. She was in her room when Stella and Anne arrived. "Merry Christmas Doc," Anne walked in with the tree and a tray of home made brownies. "Oh Anne, what have you brought?" Doc's eyes were bright with wonder just like a child. "What a beautiful tree!

Can we decorate it now?" And decorate it they did with lights and miniature ornaments. The engineering staff of the home came up and gave their seal of approval on the wiring of the cord and they plugged it in. Her room exuded a warm glow of light and with the winter sun dropping in the sky; it was a sight to behold.

"Wait, Michael and Jane sent you something as well." Stella said as she handed her a wrapped box. Doc opened it slowly and said, "Oh, it's so beautiful, a glass nativity scene." "Doc, it's a night light as well, let's plug it in." She was so excited. Nothing would do but she had to call, Stella's other children, Michael and Jane and thank each of them for remembering her with such nice gifts. Once off the phone, Doc summoned the staff to see her beautiful tree. In that moment, Doc was her old self, laughing, smiling, and sharing her fortune with everyone.

As Stella had become an almost daily visitor, some of the staff were now more comfortable in discussing Doc with her. One of the nurses said, "We were initially instructed by Jean to restrict you from visiting or phoning Doc, but we couldn't help but see how loving and kind you were to your friend." Stella thought, 'God bless the nurses for ignoring that request, always aware of what was best for a patient. They could see how Doc yearned for normalcy and Stella provided that with her visits. In addition, the staff often waited for Doc's showering and personal care until she arrived because they knew that Doc would allow Stella to help her. Stella told the staff, "Doc's memory of her first days on the unit included having a young, male nurse's aide assist her with a shower. She was mortified, and that's why she preferred having Stella help her shower."

The days that led up to Christmas were especially trying for

Doc. When visiting, Stella would ask her if she wanted to listen to music from her computer. Always the answer was yes and they would sit quietly and partake of the old Christmas carols or sing along loudly with the newer holiday songs. They made their own little reality in that small room. For fleeting bits of time, they could still enjoy one another's company and look forward to Christmas.

After dinner, Doc would oftentimes sit on the bench outside of her room, waiting to see if, when the locked unit door opened, Stella might be visiting. The room across from hers housed a patient named Gloria. Next to Gloria's doorway was a wedding photo of her and her husband, whom she no longer recognized. Gloria would sit next to Doc on the bench and repeatedly ask her who the man was in the picture. Doc was extremely annoyed with her constant questioning over the past year. A few days before Christmas, Stella arrived as Doc was sitting on the bench. She sat next to Doc and noticed the photograph across the hall was torn in half with only Gloria remaining. When Stella asked Doc what happened, she proudly said, "Gloria was always upset about the strange man and was constantly talking about it, so I tore him out of the photo." Stella thought If only all her problems could be so easily solved. Doc motioned towards her room and said, "Jean and Rita are in there." As if on cue, the door opened and Rita walked out. Stella rose and said, "Merry Christmas Rita." Winking at Doc Stella whispered, "I'll be down in the park area and come back after their visit."

Jean was fully aware that Stella was waiting and expanded her normal fifteen-minute visit to make her wait nearly two hours. When she heard them leaving, Stella walked toward Doc's room and sensed eyes staring at her. She looked towards the exit door and encountered hatred, pure unadulterated hatred, glaring from Jean's eyes. Stella decided that day to be more cautious as she could not know for certain what Jean might do. When Stella entered Doc's room, her friend was all smiles saying, "I'm so glad you stayed Stella, I thought they would never leave". "Me, too, Doc, I have news, my lawyer Vic has informed me that the court appointed guardian is coming Christmas Eve." "Good, now, maybe I can tell someone with authority that I want to go home."

When Stella left that evening, Doc was in good spirits and hopeful. Stella left a bag of small presents that Doc could give out to the staff. She was so happy to be able to give something away. When Doc asked how much was spent on the gifts, Stella lied saying she paid for it with money from Doc's account. The dollars didn't matter as it brought such joy to her friend who had a history of showering everyone with gifts.

Stella was home on Christmas Eve, preparing for her family to visit, and waited until around 5 p.m. to call Doc to ask about the guardian's visit. Doc was despondent, saying, "That person never showed up and when she does come, I will tell her to go to hell." Stella was reminded that some people simply don't care about someone locked up without cause. Damn the guardian. Why get Doc's hopes up only to have her disappointed again?

Christmas wasn't at all as it had been in the past with Stella's friend being part of their family and enjoying laughter, good food, and feeling wanted. Here again, something meaningful to Doc had been stolen from her because of a niece refusing to follow her aunt's wishes. Doc was taken out for Christmas dinner to Jean's house. While there she snuck into a bedroom and quietly called Stella, "Merry Christmas Stella" whispered Doc. "And the same to you my friend, are you enjoying your day?" Doc responded, "I'm at Jeans, it's noisy, but Rita is here and it's good to be with my sister on Christmas." "Yes, it is, wish Rita a Merry Christmas for me and I will see you tomorrow."

As the phone disconnect signal rang in Stella's ear she again pondered how life had changed this woman's ability to simply wish her friend a Merry Christmas, forcing her to sneak into a room away from listening ears. This wonderful woman had been degraded to next to nothing and for what, for what?

Stella tried to piece snippets from the past together to make sense of Doc's dilemma. Jean appeared to be her usual self throughout Doc's fall, stroke, and rehabilitation in the hospital. It wasn't until Doc recovered and was home and Jean hired Beth to watch over Doc and Rita that things began to change. It became obvious to Stella that Jean and Beth went through Doc's papers while she and Doc were away in Savannah, and discovered Doc's trust. It made sense to Stella that Jean was upset upon reading the contents of the trust. All those years of expecting that Doc would leave all her worldly possessions to Jean were dashed when she read the trust. The trust stipulated that upon Doc's death her sister Rita would be taken care of under the trusteeship of Stella. Upon Rita's death the remaining articles in the trust would be awarded to Stella. (The only article Doc inserted into the trust was the house.)

When Stella visited the next day, Doc seemed in a funky mood and didn't want to play games or sit in her room. She was restless, antsy and anxious. Stella sat with her in the lounge and they talked and sang a few songs together. She seemed much calmer as Stella was leaving and shared one of her bright smiles. Nancy, one of the nurses on the unit, approached Stella before she left and they spoke at length about Doc. "We are all wondering why Doc is here. She just doesn't belong on a locked unit."

"Nancy, I've made a rule not to talk about the circumstances surrounding Doc's incarceration, but, perhaps its time for some of this to be aired. I'm sure you have observed tension between Jean and I. There's a good reason for that tension. Doc and I had been good friends for many years, trusting friends, so, when she decided to create a legal trust, she chose me to be a trustee in charge of making sure that the trust was followed. Jean was identified as her power of attorney. As such she set out to prove that Doc could not remain in her home as the Trust detailed. She fabricated Doc's state of mind by saying that she didn't recognize anyone and was found wandering on the side of the road and didn't know how to get home.

"As you well know Doc sleeps soundly through the night and recognizes everyone."

Without my knowledge, Jean placed Doc here and removed me as trustee, so I have a legal challenge in court to reinstate me as trustee. I hope to enforce the trust, which says Doc is to remain in her home with caregivers if feasible."

Relief showed upon Stella's face because she always wanted the staff to know the real truth. Nancy was speechless. A look of total disgust crossed the nurse's face. "I see so many patients admitted and for the most part they aren't aware of their surroundings. But Doc is normal in her speech, her reactions, and it pains us to know that she is aware but can do nothing about it. I will pray for your success and if any of the staff can help, please let us know." Stella seized the opportunity to solicit her help. "There will be a court appointed guardian coming to visit Doc on Monday. If you can tell her your opinion about how Doc can function, I would be most appreciative." "You can count on me,"

Nancy happily agreed and Stella felt a sense of hope finally flowing in their direction.

Hope is an elusive but imperative part of all human experience. Stella wondered if Doc was losing hope as each day ebbed and flowed into the next. It took all of Stella's strength to keep her head above water. She helped Doc lovingly and gladly but she had her down days when everything seemed hopeless.

On New Year's Day, Jean took Doc to her home to celebrate Docs' eighty first birthday. This was wise on Jean's part as the court-appointed guardian was due to visit Doc that week. It was important to present as a caring niece to the courts in order to appear credible. Doc called Stella from Jean's house and said, "Can you hear me? I have to whisper, I don't want them to know I called you. I'm so tired Stella, no-one bothers to even talk to me, I just want to go back to the unit." "Oh Doc, I'm glad you called, Happy Birthday, my friend. Hang in there, they will take you back soon and I'll see you tonight."

Lately, she seemed to be even more ill at ease whenever she was around Jean. She confided in Stella, "When Jean is here, I don't complain anymore because she is running the show and I'm afraid of what might happen." "What more could she do that she hasn't already done?" "She could admit me into a psychiatric ward." Stella went to visit Doc around five p.m. bringing fudge her daughter had made for her. It didn't take much to make Doc happy. She loved chocolate and loved Stella's daughter and so, with those two things combined, Doc was in heaven.

Jolene, the court appointed guardian for Doc, interviewed her on January third. According to the report that Stella's attorney shared, Doc knew her name at the end of the meeting, knew where she was, knew the date, knew where her home was, and referred to Jean as the traitor. Ha! Well, that said it all. Her attorney informed Stella that an independent case manager would also assess Doc's ability to be cared for in her own home. Strangers would now decide her fate.

Before Stella spoke with her attorney, she called the unit and spoke with Nancy. "How did the meeting with the guardian work out? Was Doc calm and able to answer her questions?" "Unfortunately, we were given the directive to not speak with the guardian since there was a legal case pending. But I think it went okay, as Doc seemed to be in a good mood. If all goes well with your case, will you be the one caring for Doc if she is able to go home?"

Stella responded, "That's unlikely since the family would still be in charge." Stella's focus had always been to release Doc from a locked unit and bring her home. Whether the family would allow her to visit at Doc's home was now in question.

Stella spent most of January in her home in Savannah. She talked with Doc on the phone every day. The nurses never stopped Doc when she reached through the window of the nurse's station for the phone. At times, Doc would call two or three times a day. She was an open book when it came to whatever was on her mind. No mincing of words with her! Stella could hear in her voice if she was scared or agitated, and knew that some days were very difficult for Doc. Stella tried to reassure her that the time would pass quickly and then she would be home. While in Savannah, she contemplated paying extra money to change her airline ticket and return home but she forced herself to stay, knowing she needed to refresh herself physically and mentally for the battle awaiting them. When Stella arrived home, she went to see Doc immediately. She hadn't told Doc that she would visit the same day of her return, so when she walked in, Doc began to cry.

They held onto each other and Stella realized how her life and Doc's were inexplicably bound together. While in Savannah, Stella had an old picture of the two of them sitting in Stella's rose garden enjoying their morning coffee, transferred onto a sweatshirt. Underneath the picture was written "My Buddy." Stella handed it to Doc and she had to put it on right then and there. Grinning from ear to ear, she mirrored the picture she wore. After putting it on, she requested that Stella get her two more in different colors so she could wear them all the time.

In future visits, Doc's demeanor changed. At first, Stella thought Doc seemed more peaceful but that was not really accurate. More often than not, Doc was quiet during their visits and sat looking off into the distance. When asked what she was thinking about, Doc usually replied, "Oh nothing" or "You really don't want to know." Stella suspected that Doc was depressed and used every ounce of energy she could muster to keep her in their world and not allow her to be absorbed into the snake pit surrounding her. Doc continued to refer to herself as a prisoner and said she had to get out of the viper's den or explode. On one occasion, Stella realized that Doc might have been considering suicide when she asked Stella to pack up all the stuffed animals that graced her bed and give them away. These were animals that she coveted, given to her by Stella and friends. "Stella, take the animals home with you." "Why Doc, you loved them and you certainly liked lifting a few off of other people's beds." Stella said with a laugh. "Just take them, I have no use for them," Was Doc's only response.

An eerie feeling stole into Stella's thoughts, could Doc be

contemplating suicide? The thought hit her like a ton of bricks. Suicide? It was hard to imagine such a thought from a woman who talked to her guardian angel and prayed fervently to our Father in heaven every day. How despondent and depressed she must have felt if she would ever contemplate such an act. Being in that situation was a form of torture. No need to water board, just keep someone locked up with the gnawing realization that it may be forever. Stella debated with herself about informing the staff of the change she noticed in Doc but she knew that Jean would use that information against Doc to keep her where she wanted her. Stella vowed to be more vigilant in assessing Doc's state of mind.

In addition to seeing Doc's depression and worrying about her, Stella was given a report from the independent source who had evaluated Doc's ability to live at home with assistance. Stella, through Vic, had requested the evaluation and Jean and her attorney approved, but the report was fundamentally flawed. Where the evaluator should have assessed Doc's current condition both physically and emotionally, the report drew in assessments of her sister Rita as well as their financial status. It was apparent that Jean and her lawyer had handpicked this evaluator and that the conclusions were drawn from a source other than Doc. The information was erroneous even to the point of having the evaluation state that Doc used a wheelchair. Stella immediately sent a response on this flawed and biased report to her attorney. Ultimately, that report would work in her favor as the judge would also question the scope of the report.

Stella was scheduled to return to Savannah for the month of March and visited Doc to tell her of the plans. Sitting in her room, Doc looked up and said, "I will miss you Stella, but I want you to rest and enjoy yourself. You do so much for me and I can't do anything for you. I'm sad but I will call you everyday. You know the nurses always let me call." Yes, they are so good about that. What would we do if we couldn't talk each day? Doc, have I ever told you how much your friendship means to my family and me? When I get sad I think about all the holidays, the wonderful trips we've taken, especially the one to Mexico City and just the day to day laughs we've enjoyed." Doc's face lit up as she said, "I wish we could go on just one more adventure." To which Stella told her the only trip she wanted to plan was the one to take her home. They listened to classical music and Stella reminded her to pray very hard for her special intention. Doc replied that it was all going to work out.

On February twenty eighth, Stella went to court and seated herself behind her lawyer, Jean's lawyer and Doc's court appointed lawyer. She was privy to their discussion about her request to have Doc reevaluated for home care. Jean's lawyer stated that Stella would have to pay for the reevaluation, as Doc's estate money was getting low. Then Jean's lawyer said, in an imperial tone, "Perhaps you should contact her and explain the cost of the re-evaluation and see if she would be willing to incur the additional cost?" Stella's lawyer said, "She's right behind you. I'll ask her now." Jean's lawyer was not pleased and said that it could all be a moot point if the judge decided that Stella had no standing in the case. Doc's guardian lawyer stated firmly that she had reviewed the trust thoroughly and didn't believe the judge would rule against Stella. This was the second time that Stella felt a real glimmer of hope. The judge indeed supported another impartial party to evaluate Doc for home care and set another date in court for March seventeenth.

What a joyous visit Doc and Stella had that day. She brought Doc coffee and brownies that Anne had made for her. Doc was in seventh heaven and smiled broadly when Stella said, "Things are looking up Doc. It may be possible to get you home. One more person is coming to talk with you regarding home care." Doc was sincerely happy. Stella was once again going away for a few weeks to her home in Savanna. "Doc we're getting to the end of the journey and I know you've been patient, but I need you to be on your best behavior, don't lose your temper and please be cooperative with the staff." "Scouts honor, I'll be good and I'll call you three times a day."

My goodness, how the roles have changed. Doc was always there to encourage Stella, never letting her waiver in attaining advanced degrees. Now Stella was there for Doc, trying to give her back her life.

Doc was true to her word calling three times every day and Stella aimed at keeping her on the phone, as she knew she lacked interaction with anyone, except the staff. There definitely was no interaction with the other patients. God help them, they were living, but not alive. Doc shared with Stella that when Rita visited she watched television or enjoyed cookies and juice as if she were a resident. She also said that when Jean accompanied Rita, she was reluctant to talk with her sister.

While in Savannah, Stella's lawyer called and said the re-evaluation was scheduled for March eleventh. Stella told Doc about the date when she called and kept reiterating that she should be herself and not to worry. This must have weighed heavily on Doc's mind because every phone call until the eleventh was full of angst and anxiety about the evaluation. Finally, on that day, Doc called while Stella was driving up to the mountains. Up there, the reception is rarely available or very bad, but Stella's guardian angels were working overtime because she could hear Doc as if she were seated next to her. She said that the lady came and asked her silly questions like "Could I brush my own teeth, and wash and clothe myself?" Doc said the lady said, as she was leaving, "You passed." "What does that mean?" Doc asked. "Can I come home now?"

The court hearing to decide if Stella could remain as trustee took place as scheduled on March seventeenth, St. Patrick's feast day. She tried to keep herself busy, as she was very nervous about the decision. So much depended upon this judgment. If Doc were to live out her life in her own home among her own things and enjoying the peacefulness that accompanied that, the verdict would have to be in Stella's favor. Otherwise, Jean would win and Doc would remain in a locked environment. Stella knew the hearing was in the morning, so when she had not heard from her lawyer as promised by three p.m., anxiety and stress descended upon her. She was frantic. Why hadn't he called? Everywhere Stella looked, the image of Doc sitting in the unit haunted her. Finally, around 5:30 p.m., he called and said that Jean was not successful in removing Stella as trustee. He said it without much emotion but Stella was jumping for joy! Finally, a decision had been made! She was legally recognized as the trustee! She now had a say in what happened to her friend! Along with the court's ruling came a question regarding the report from the evaluating agency and the cost of home care. Good God, what next? Stella had to talk to herself to keep a positive mood, telling herself that they had come a long way but it appeared there was still a way to go. Stella had already completed a list and given it to Vic that identified and detailed the worth of Doc's financially secure investments. Stella's expert accounting showed that Doc had more than enough funds to keep her safely and comfortably in her own home.

One evening Doc called Stella to thank her for the Hershey bars when Stella suddenly heard Doc call out, "Help, help, get this person away from me." Doc was urgently trying to get the attention of the staff as one of the patients was attacking her. It took a few moments for the staff to calm the patient down and then Doc said, "I have to get out of here! " The urgency in her voice was a clear warning that if she remained there, she could possibly be hurt or hurt someone else.

Upon returning from Savannah, Stella visited Doc the first thing in the morning with coffee and a sweet roll. Doc looked disheveled with dirty hair, nails, and clothes. Stella washed her face and neck, clipped her fingernails, and put clean clothes on her before giving her a good back rub and massaging her hands with cream. Doc said she was happy Stella was back. Stella felt the same. She felt energetic and able to face the future, come what may.

Every day began with concern for Doc's well being. Stella often thought, is this the day that Doc's faith fails her? Is this the day she gives into despair? Is this the day all of her pent-up feelings explode? Stella wondered what would happen if she was not around to pull her back from the dark abyss and into the living world?

Stella spent the better part of the next day with Doc. "Doc, are you tired?" Stella noticed that Doc appeared very groggy. She slipped off into a sound sleep and slept for an hour. This was unusual for Doc as she always relished her visits with Stella. She was in a sound sleep when Stella walked to the nurse's station saw the nurse Nancy, and inquired about what medications had been administered prior to her visit. "I think she is being over medicated with Tylenol #3. Jean requested the Doctor to increase the medication from once daily to three times a day." "Well, I think you should notify the doctor that it is making Doc very lethargic, don't you?" "Yes, I'll document that and pass it on in report. We will try to get it changed to whenever Doc says she's in pain instead of three times a day." It was obvious that the increased medication was dulling her senses and making her very sleepy. Upon her awakening, Stella and Doc talked and played "Deal or No Deal" and "Who Wants to be a Millionaire?" Doc came up with many of the correct answers. As the day wore on, Stella read the newspaper out loud. In a quiet moment, Doc shared that she believed she would get released one way or another. The last part of that statement concerned Stella as she wondered if Doc succumbed to feeling that all was lost, she might abscond. Doc knew the code to release the door and she had shown Stella how the alarm bracelet could be slipped off of her wrist, so Stella knew she had the ability to leave undetected. Stella made a mental note to always leave Doc with thoughts of hope and ask her to patiently pray for a good outcome.

CHAPTER 11

Request for Dissolution of Guardianship

Doc was seated in the hallway and stared off into space. She was barely aware that Stella had come to visit. Her eyes appeared lifeless and Stella's heart skipped in her chest. She tried to get Doc interested in playing a game or listening to music but Doc was in a funky mood so they just sat in the lounge and talked and sang a few songs together.

During recent visits, Stella noticed Doc's increased napping and realized that sleeping her day away was the mechanism that she used to simply get through the day and allow time to pass. In addition, Doc had been shielding her left eye with her hand, leading Stella to believe that she was experiencing increased pain in her eye. Doc had her eye monitored every six months by an Ophthalmologist until Jean assumed responsibility for her care. During those visits, treatments and medication to reduce the inflammation in the eye were administered. After Jean took over she did not follow this routine. She did however request that Stella take Doc to have her eye assessed by a Radiologist, a friend of Jean's. His specialty was in the area of radiation treatment for tumors. After the examination his recommendation was to either remove the eye or do a series of radiation treatments to reduce the tumor. Doc refused both suggestions. Ironically, a year later that physician was one of the two physicians who signed a document stating that Doc was unable to handle her finances or make medical decisions, thus allowing Jean to sign Doc's liberty away. In looking back, Stella believed that visit to the Radiologist was planned by Jean so that he could later be asked to sign a declaration of Doc's competency. Seeing Doc in pain was agonizing to Stella. How she wished that she had a legal right to demand a follow-up with the eye specialist.

Easter was just days away. In the church calendar, this time of year was most meaningful especially in Doc's ethnic community. They had wonderful traditions that included the Holy Saturday blessing of baskets with food to be used in their holiday dinner. On Easter morning, a procession of priests, altar boys, and the congregation circle the church three times in procession while the organ plays for the first time since having been silenced on Good Friday. During mass at the recitation of the Gloria prayer, the church bells peal in joy. After mass, everyone returns to their homes to eat the blessed foods. Stella was sure that Doc was remembering past Easters and feeling a little sad at the prospect of not being home to celebrate this year.

Stella was with Doc on Holy Saturday and witnessed her face light up with joy when Anne walked in with Ginger, her pup, and a large Easter basket filled with goodies. "Hi Doc, I've brought someone who's been missing you." Anne said as she placed Ginger on the floor. The dog ran immediately to Doc jumping up on her hind legs with her tail wagging. "Oh Anne, thank you, I've missed her so much." Doc was so excited; it did Stella's heart good to see a fully natural response of love coming from her friend. Ginger was beside herself, leaping up onto Doc's lap and staying there for the entire visit, enjoying each stroke that Doc lovingly placed. Specks of normalcy were brought into Doc's life just when she needed it the most.

Stella was in limbo. She had gained recognition as the trustee in the eyes of the court but was still praying that the courts would review all aspects of Doc's ability, especially financial, to be cared for in her home. Doc's quality of life was now resting in the hands of judges, a court-appointed guardian, and a social worker.

It was during this phase that the court asked Jean, Doc's guardian, to submit the required annual financial report detailing Doc's finances for review by the judge. According to Stella's attorney, there were discrepancies discovered in the report. Either through poor bookkeeping or misappropriation of funds, a substantial amount of Doc's estate money was missing. Jean was asked to provide the court with an acceptable explanation of all financial transactions related to Doc's assets since Jean became her guardian.

Easter had come and gone. It was nearly one year since Doc was kidnapped and brought to the nursing home. Stella wondered which year of Jean's life would she be willing to have snatched from her? Doc had lost precious time being locked up. At eighty-one years of age, time truly does become "of the essence." Every day, every sunrise and sunset, every visit with those we love, every moment of beauty and music is savored. Humans are on borrowed time and have a need to drink it all in. It was so sad that Doc's remaining time had been limited in its possibilities.

Since the weather cooperated, Stella took Doc outside to sit by the entrance so that she could hear outside sounds, see people coming and going, and generally feel a part of life again. The front door faced a parking lot and wasn't nearly as pleasant as the beautiful garden in the center of the building. Doc truly enjoyed the activity of people coming and going. Just being out of the locked unit made Doc smile and feel alive. One-day Stella used the time to tell Doc about the trip to Europe she had planned with her friends. "It's going to be a long trip Doc We'll start out in Rome and work our way north to Lucca which is in Tuscany. Then we will pick up a cruise coming out of Civitavecchia. That will take us to Greece, Croatia and Santorini. It's going to be so wonderful Doc." Doc was listening but didn't appear to be engaged in the conversation. Finally, Stella said, "We'll talk more about this later, it will be ok, and I have a plan for when we can talk every day." "You will have a beautiful time with your buddies, but I will miss you", Doc said as she patted Stella's hand. They would be away for nearly a month and she was concerned that Doc would lose ground without their daily interactions. Thinking ahead, she had begun to read a few chapters every day from interesting books to her, hoping to exercise her mind. One of the books was "The Wishing Well." Doc knew the characters and laughed at all the right places. God, Stella loved to hear her robust laugh!

June flew by and July was half over. The warm, sunny weather seemed to have perked Doc up. Early in the month Jean was spotted, standing outside of Doc's house speaking to a man that arrived with a truck. Shortly thereafter, he began to remove pieces of furniture from the truck and place them inside Doc's house. From where Stella stood they looked like secondhand mismatched sofa and chairs. Why was this happening? Was Jean ordered by the court to return everything back to the house? This begged the question, where did all of Doc's furniture and personal assets go? Did Jean sell everything? Did Doc's possessions end up in Jean's home, or her sister's, or in the home of a stranger? Where were the expensive paintings? Stella called Vic. "Jean is next door with a man and a rental truck. I've been watching furniture being brought back into Doc's house, has something happened that I should know about?" "I believe that Jean is running scared. Apparently, the financial report she submitted to the court didn't ring true except in her greediness, as she paid herself handsomely for her duties." Vic went on to tell her, "Just keep an eye out and let me know if anything out of the ordinary is happening."

What we become in our lifetime, how we treat others, and what our deepest and truest feelings are will somehow make their way onto our faces. Mother Theresa is what many would consider homely but when you look upon her, there is a kindness and softness in her face which portrays the true essence of her being. With Jean, everything she did and thought was painted on her face for all to see. Stella recognized this one day while sitting outside with Doc. Jean arrived to drop off Rita and when she looked at Doc, with a wide maniacal smile, it was as if a crazed person was now inhabiting Jean.

Doc appeared more improved every day with her trips outside to sit in the sunshine and interact with others. Visitors and staff stopped to say hello to Doc and why not? She was always smiling. Remembering those times, Stella truly believed that Jean was counting on Doc deteriorating quickly and perhaps dying. This is not to say that Jean wished that upon her, she simply had no faith in Doc's ability to hang onto her wonderful mind. What a shame, Stella often wondered, has any good come out of this heartache?

Stella noticed on those occasions when both she and Jean were present on the unit together, there was a palpable feeling of hatred. It appeared difficult for Jean to cope with being in close proximity to Stella. Jean usually turned on her heels and headed for the door. She either despised Stella intensely or was ashamed of what she had done. Or, most likely, a little bit of both.

The end of July brought the symphony back to the grounds of the nursing home. Stella had arranged to bring her sister and two of her grandchildren to hear the concert with Doc, but Jean had come earlier and took Doc to sit with her family. Stella was disappointed but sought out Doc at intermission and was able to speak to her briefly. She realized that in the end, no matter with whom she sat, Doc truly loved the music.

Early in August, Stella received a phone call from Vic to be in court on August ninth. He said the words that were beyond Stella's greatest expectation. "Jean will be petitioning the court to approve her stepping down as Doc's guardian. Are you ready to accept the role of guardian?" Stella was stunned but responded "Yes, of course." She was, holding the phone to her ear, pacing back and forth. She recognized this as a turning point in her case. She had secretly feared that even if the courts directed Jean to return Doc to her home, she might never be able to be with her friend if Jean retained guardianship and forbade her from contact.

On August ninth, Stella arrived at the court with her sister for support. If all went well at the court hearing, there would begin the unraveling of the horrible nightmare that entrapped her dear friend and restricted her every movement! The long awaited moment slipped into the court proceedings without fanfare. Jean's lawyer pleaded with the court. "My client is requesting to be released from her duties as guardian due to the increased stress that is affecting her life. She is overwhelmed and cannot continue to care for her family, her medical practice and guardianship of her aging aunt."

If stress can be said to change the look of a person, then perhaps Jean was accurate in her request, for she looked like hell and appeared to have aged ten years. The court accepted Jean's petition. Vic then approached the bench.

"If it pleases the court, my client is requesting that you consider her request for guardianship pending the necessary completion and filing of paper work." One more step towards our goal.

For the first time, Stella decided to speak with Doc after the proceedings and update her on what had occurred. She found her sitting outside her room on one of the benches alone with her hands folded on her lap. Looking up she smiled as Stella joined her on the bench. After a little bit of small talk, Stella said, "Doc, you know how I always ask you to pray for a special intention. Well, I have been praying that everything will work out. My lawyer has been petitioning the court to get you out of here. I haven't told you up to this point because I didn't want to get your hopes up." "I knew Stella what that special intention was." They sat side by side for a while and Stella thought that Doc's affect seemed a little flat. She observed that the longer Doc remained on the unit, signs of resignation to being there appeared, and that worried her and spurred her on to return Doc to her home as quickly as possible.

"We need prayers to accomplish this Doc. Please continue to pray for a good outcome." "I will pray to St. Jude and Our Blessed Mother." As she left the unit, Stella's heart was filled with hope but she was cautiously optimistic and not counting her chickens before they hatched.

The papers for guardianship were completed at Vic's office. Who would have thought that the road to Doc's release, with all its twists and turns, would finally see a long-awaited moment of sunshine stream through? Days came and went much as before but Stella had become patient, something that she never envisioned for herself. She was always the one tapping her finger or toe as if that would hurry a process along. Now, she quietly laid everything in God's hands and realized that the courts move at a snail's pace and she would have to wait, regardless of her inner turmoil.

Stella's month-long trip to Italy involved much planning about Doc. Friends of Doc and Stella were enlisted to call her daily and visit if possible. During the cruise and while traveling on land, Stella called Doc who would be waiting by the nurse's station, around dinnertime, as previously discussed. Carrying on a long-distance relationship is difficult but in Doc's case, it was imperative to sustain the lifeline she desperately needed.

When she returned from her trip, Stella visited Doc only to find her profoundly withdrawn and not walking as well as before the trip. Sitting in her room, she had no spark in her eyes nor did she interact with Stella other than to say yes or no. According to the nurses, "Doc only comes out of her room to eat. Occasionally she sits on the bench outside her room. We've been worried about her and we're so glad you are back."

Doc's regression was a bit of a shock to Stella who did not foresee that it would happen so quickly. She began a one-woman campaign to get her back to square one, beginning with her hygiene. She knew that the staff considered Doc a self-help patient but her fingernails, toenails, hair, and whole body was sorely in need of a good cleaning and clipping. Stella began with her nails, clipping and filing until they looked normal.

She also made sure that the podiatrist who once a month

would come to clip the patients' toenails evaluated Doc. When he attended Doc, Stella made sure she was there so that she could point out that, near a bunion on one of her feet, was a sore. He didn't particularly care about Stella's observations, but he did order medication to be applied daily to that area. Stella was so distressed over his degree of cleanliness it took everything for her to keep her mouth closed. He used the small kitchen area where some of the residents ate their meals to clip and buff down their nails with a drill. While doing so, clouds of debris were floating up into the air. Stella never observed any additional cleaning of the room after he completed his treatments. Did he even clean his instruments between patients? Stella had to stop herself from taking on this problem as there were bigger fish to fry and one of the biggest questions was why her friend, who supposedly was taking a shower, still did not look clean? Stella asked the staff "Please let me know when Doc is scheduled for a shower so that I can be here to assist her." The staff followed her request and gave her the day and time of her next shower. Stella came away from that experience wetter than Doc but at least she had been soaped and rinsed and smelled good. The shower room was very cold and that could be one reason why Doc hurried the whole process and did a limited wash. Stella also requested that a wound care nurse evaluate Doc's feet. After meeting with the wound nurse Stella washed and provided the prescribed treatment daily. The sore appeared to be healing, and Stella helped to reduce the irritation to the area by having Doc's gym shoes stretched, especially in the area of the bunion. All in all, Doc seemed to have less discomfort with the introduction of a simple measure.

During this time, Stella found it odd that Rita was no longer visiting "Doc, when was the last time Rita was here to visit?" "She hasn't been here for a long time." Thinking this was odd, Stella walked down to the nursing station. The nurses and aides were getting ready to bring the patients to the dining room for dinner when she asked. "Have any of you seen Rita, Doc's sister, visiting within the last month?" The nursing staff confirmed that Rita's visits stopped concurrent with the time Stella left for her trip to Europe. Stella began to wonder if Rita had become ill, placed into a nursing home or, God forbid, died. She checked the obituaries and then sought out the priest for the facility and asked him if Doc had still been attending mass with her sister and niece. He replied that she hadn't been coming to the Saturday evening mass since her sister moved away one month ago. Following up on their conversation, Stella, ever the investigator began to make phone calls to the local nursing homes, but to no avail. No one had a Rita Sliwa as a client. A few weeks later, Stella spoke with the priest again and he said he had received a note from Rita. This didn't surprise Stella as Rita was beyond religious and felt comfort in knowing every nun and priest in the neighborhood and communicating with them. The note contained her address, thank God. Stella told the priest she would like to write to her so he shared the address. She was in a skilled nursing home run by nuns. It was evident that all of this was done without advising her sister Doc. Jean laid yet another layer of abandonment upon Doc by stripping away even the visits with her sister. It was no wonder that Doc slipped into such a desperate condition while Stella was away.

CHAPTER 12

Prayers Answered

October arrived and with it a phone call from Vic. "Just to keep you updated Stella, Jean's written request to abdicate her guardianship and your petition to become Doc's guardian have been submitted to the court." "That's good news Vic, now we get to play the waiting game, right?" "Yes, but it also gives us time to have all our ducks in a row. Your chances are good providing that another member of Doc's family does not request guardianship. Pretty much the court will accept her request to end her role as guardian. In any instance lets keep our fingers crossed." "I have everything possible crossed Vic, please keep updating me, it keeps me off the edge." "Right, talk to you when I have anything more to report. In the meantime, keep calm."

Stella continued to see Doc every day executing their routine that kept Doc clean and filled her day with activity. Taking Doc to the shower room was abandoned for sponge baths in her room where it was warmer and there was more privacy. During one of the baths, Stella noted a skin breakdown in Doc's lower back and asked the nurses to have the wound specialist assess it. At the end of those days when she saw Doc spit spot clean she realized that caring for her dearest friend had become very personal to her, she felt the same sense of fulfillment that she experienced as a new nurse.

Stella spoke with Vic as often as he would return her calls. He gave her hope and strength that all would work out well. At the end of October, Stella arrived at court with her stomach churning and every nerve in her body under strict orders to remain calm. After what seemed an eternity, she was informed that a final decision would be made regarding her petition for guardianship on December eighth. Until that time, Stella was given permission to take Doc out of the facility under her care during the day. This was an encouraging sign, as it showed that the courts had placed their trust in her.

Stella immediately went from court to Doc, handing the official statement of the court to the nursing staff. She literally bounced down the hallway of the Alzheimer's unit with the biggest grin on her face. Stella listened to the happy nurses as they said, "We told Jean that Doc did not belong here in a locked unit. From the first day of admission our assessment indicated that she should be moved to a skilled nursing unit." Jean didn't listen to anyone, continuing her quest to be the almighty expert and saying Doc would find it difficult to be uprooted twice and that she would most likely elope. Jean would not agree to a skilled nursing unit for Doc because the standard of care in that type of unit would be the same as caring for Doc in her own home with assistance. That would have supported the condition of the trust that she be cared for at home if feasible. Stella dismissed those thoughts and said, "Well, this is a day of joy and I can't wait to tell Doc that we are going out." There were so many wonderful moments that day. Stella knocked on Doc's door, opened it and said, "Doc, let's get you dressed, I have a surprise for you. I'm taking you out for the day!" Stella was standing there with a wide smile and Doc returned it with a grin from ear to ear. A quick bath, clean clothes and hair combed, and they were off for five glorious hours. Moments of bringing her back to Stella's house and having her visit with members of her family could never be recaptured. Stella's face should have ached from the constant smile it needed to support. Doc told everyone "I've been let out of jail."

Tears were in everyone's eyes, tears of joy and relief.

"No matter how dark the night, morning always comes ... and our journey begins anew."
   Final Fantasy X111

The next morning, Stella went to Doc, helping her to dress as they were going to take a ride to see Rita, whom she missed so much. The weather was cold and the walkways were icy at the nursing home. Walking slowly, they stood at the front door only to find it locked. "Don't worry Doc, I'll call and try to get someone to answer the door." She was undaunted and used her cell phone to repeatedly call the nursing home. Finally, one of the good sisters came to the door and walked with them to Rita's room, saying "Rita is having her hair done and will join you soon. Make yourself comfortable." When Rita did arrive, there was a look of shock upon her face. She started to cry and talked a mile a minute. The two sisters, in their eighties had not spoken for months, both worried about each other. Now they sat in chairs next to each other, holding hands and laughing. Rita said, "This is the best Christmas present ever." What a wonderful visit. All the way back to the unit, Doc repeated Rita's name and profusely thanked Stella. Walking back on the unit, she told everyone that she had seen her sister. It had been a long time since Stella saw Doc so animated and happy. The next day, two of Stella's friends accompanied Stella, picked up Doc and went to a family restaurant so that Doc could enjoy her favorite waffles and ice cream. When they were seated and the waitress was taking their order, Doc smiled at her and said, "I just got out of prison." The look on the waitress's face was classic! A picture was taken of Doc that day that showed the biggest smile on her face and life in her eyes as she sat and ate not one but two orders of ice cream and waffles.

Doc and Stella's prayers were again answered on the Blessed Mother's feast day of the Immaculate Conception, December eighth. This was the same date as Doc's hip surgery two years previously. Stella was officially named Doc's guardian and Jean was removed as power of attorney. It all seemed to go so quickly. Stella was ecstatic. She wanted to rush forward and kiss the judge for beginning the dismantling of this nightmare. Following the court's decision, in the hallway, Jean's attorney approached Stella with a binder filled with Doc' s financial history. "You have a real hard job ahead of you. I wish you well Stella," as the lawyer handed her a binder which contained the court required final financial accounting by Jean as Doc's guardian. Also included was a certified check from Jean for $50,000 paid to the order of Doc's Estate. This was a payback mandated by the court upon their review of Jean's disbursements from Doc's accounts. Though this was just a small portion of the money that was unaccounted for, Stella did not question the sum, as she did not want to provoke more problems with Jean.

Stella went directly to see Doc and told her the good news, saying over and over, "I can't believe it." Sobbing for the first time in many months, Stella fully experienced tears of joy.

The following day Stella entered Doc's house for the first time in over two years. She knew this house as she knew her own, like the back of her hand. It was shockingly apparent that most of Doc's personal items were missing. The beautiful oil paintings that once graced her walls, were replaced with cheap copy prints Her piano and living room furniture were no where to be found, all gone, replaced with second hand store merchandise with nothing matching. When Stella entered Doc's bedroom, her jewelry box no longer contained the quality jewelry she enjoyed wearing. In its place was an assortment of costume jewelry rings and items Doc would never have purchased.

Stella took pictures and videotaped all of the contents in the house, proceeding to itemize the missing items and their approximate worth. This was not difficult as she had pictures of most of the contents from years past. Stella also contacted the interior decorator, Doc hired to furnish her home before she moved in, asking for an approximate cost of the furnishings. Stella then sent Vic the video pictures and estimates of all items. After receiving Stella's photo's, Video and proofs of purchase Vic said, "I'll file a petition for restitution Stella". He was incredulous that so much of Doc's personal property had been sold, given away, thrown away or whatever. Subsequent to this petition, Jean was ordered by the court to give a deposition regarding the unaccounted personal property of Docs'. At the deposition Jean was asked to prove why it was necessary to remove and dispose all personal items of Doc's, including her furniture, paintings, and jewelry. Stella was in attendance and it was obvious to all that Jean was unable to give an honest account, contradicting herself several times when explaining what happened to the contents of the house.

Stella's next task was to enlist her friends to help her ready Doc's home for her return. The house was given a thorough cleaning, new pictures were hung, some new furniture was bought, carpets were cleaned which made the house once again look like a real home. In addition, her friends helped restock the pantry, wash dishes, and purchase any small appliance or utensil needed to cook in the kitchen.

Stella did everything from purchasing an elevated toilet with grab bars at the side to providing extra lighting in any dimly lit area to make Doc's home safe for her return. Once the house was readied Stella concentrated on reintegrating Doc into Stella's family and her previous life. Most days, Stella took her off the unit, brought her home, or took her shopping or out to eat. Stella had planned a short trip to Savannah and was contemplating not going until she realized how much of a toll this experience had taken on her. A visit away would give her the rest and recuperation she sorely needed prior to returning Doc to her home.

CHAPTER 13

Home Sweet Home

The day of Doc's return held so many wonderful moments. Her face showed pure joy as she said good-bye to the nursing staff and shouted to everyone, "I'm going home." This was indeed a first for this unit as virtually nobody ever returned home after being placed there, the nurse said, "All the nurses from the three shifts went out last night to celebrate Doc's impending discharge and offered a toast to friendship. We are so happy that after eighteen months she can finally go home."

Stella took in every moment of Doc's leaving; beginning at the locked gray door and ending at the front entrance and burned it into her memory. Never again would she have to see her friend standing in that window, waving her tissue box and blowing kisses. She, at last, was taking her home where she belonged.

Once home, Doc appeared confused, saying, "Is this my home?" Although the exterior of the house was unchanged, the interior lacked familiar possessions that she may have remembered, "Where is my piano, Stella?" "Your furniture was replaced, but this is still your home" Over time, Stella would see that Doc once again remembered her home, and felt safe and secure there.

In order to give Doc a sense of ease with her surroundings, Stella spent the first month with Doc in her home. It was an adjustment for Doc but she felt safe with Stella near her and soon there were signs of healing. Stella recognized that a full-time live-in caretaker would be needed. Fearful that Doc would become totally dependent on her, she began her search for the perfect caretaker, one who would be accepted by Doc. The task of hiring someone was difficult. Initially, Stella researched different agencies, wanting to know if they were legitimate, if they did background checks of their employees, and their fees. When contacting agencies Stella always informed them that she wished to interview the caretakers. The owner of one of the agencies, who was a woman, said there was no need to do this as they would send someone and, if after a few days Doc didn't like the caretaker, the agency would come and pick them up. Stella said this would not be an option and insisted upon interviewing candidates. The agent agreed and arranged to bring someone to the house for Stella to interview. Stella had Doc present so she could observe whom she appeared to be comfortable with and Stella likewise wanted the caregiver to have an opportunity to see whom they would be caring for. Wasn't she surprised when the agent brought three people for her to interview together? Though in Stella's previous profession she had interviewed and hired hundreds of people, she didn't quite know how to handle this scenario. They all sat on the couch next to each other. As Stella directed the first question to the candidates, she took notes for future reference. "Tell me please, each of you, when you last worked and your responsibilities.

The first candidate was a woman in her fifties, with hair pulled back in a bun. She wore glasses and was dressed in a winter wool suit, dark brown with gold buttons down the front. She had on very sensible black oxford shoes. From what Stella could understand, she was a teacher back in Poland and while working in the States she only cared for patients fluent in polish.

Although Doc could speak fluent Polish, Stella wanted a caretaker with whom she could communicate. The second candidate was tall, thin, in her forties who was very vocal about duties that she did not feel were in her job description. She mentioned several times that she required paid weekends off. 'Hmmm' thought Stella, this one has an awful lot of what she won't do and a little of what she will do. The third candidate was elderly and found it difficult to keep her eyes open during the interview. "Well, thank you ladies for the frank answers to my questions, I will be in contact with the agency if one of you is selected." When it came time for them to leave, the elderly candidate had a hard time getting up and Doc, the one who was to be taken care of, got off the couch to help her, saying," Let me help you."

What was wrong with this picture thought Stella? Neither satisfied nor even the slightest bit interested in any of the candidates, Stella severed any further dealings with that agency. In thinking about the unique requirements for this position, Stella included someone who could drive and had access to a car. That would relieve Stella of having to do grocery shopping and other errands, and would afford the caregiver some time during Stella's daily visit to be away from the home and mentally refresh herself. Stella personally checked and verified the credentials of the caretakers, checked references, and talked with the families they worked for in the past. Stella asked questions of the candidates and the previous families they worked for, related to their temperament, and cooking and cleaning skills but most importantly, she asked about the actual care they provided and about their experience in taking care of people with similar difficulties. Stella provided specific scenarios, asking how they would handle or diffuse the situations. After interviewing many agencies and caretakers, Stella selected Elena, who remained until the very end of Doc's life.

Elena began working within a few days and Stella remained in Docs home for two weeks to assist Doc with this transition. Doc soon realized that Elena would joyfully serve her ice cream every hour on the hour until Doc replaced that craving with another, like coffee. Elena took a long weekend off every other week, during which time Stella stayed with her good friend. For the two remaining years of Doc's life, the same wonderful caretaker took excellent care of her.

As Doc's eyesight lessened, a larger television with better definition was purchased. She enjoyed the game shows and they were a great source of stimulation. Her face lit up when she knew the correct answer. Watching movies became difficult since they required too much concentration, but she lived for the reruns of old television shows like Lawrence Welk and she sang along at the top of her voice. Stella remembered the old Doc and how she loved wearing bright colors so she bought colorful comfortable shirts and pajamas. Before leaving at night, Stella would bring several outfits to show Doc and ask her which one she wanted to wear the next day. The selected combination of pants and shirt would be left out for Elena to dress Doc in the morning. A beautician came to her home to give her a permanent when needed so that she would feel better about herself. She loved when friends and other visitors would tell her how good she looked

Elena and Stella conversed daily with Doc, keeping her stimulated and alert. A calendar was placed at her bedside and every day, an X was drawn over the previous day so she could keep track of days passing. A very large decorative clock was placed on the wall next to the television so she would know the time. It also served another purpose. Keeping Elena sane as Doc had begun asking, "what time is it?" every few minutes.

Things progressed nicely in Doc's new household. She and Stella attended church on Sundays, occasionally going afterward to the casino with friends. Doc blossomed during this time. Visits from friends kept her spirits up and made her feel important. One of the friends acquired later in her life was a woman named Terry who met Doc through the bank when she purchased her home ten years prior. Terry took a special liking to Doc and visited almost daily. Terry brought joy and a sense of normalcy to the household. Stella wondered if it was Terry Doc so looked forward to or the goodies she brought to share, as Doc rarely declined a muffin or sweet. She always felt loved and special when Terry visited.

The first Christmas after she returned to her home, a beautiful artificial flocked Christmas tree was assembled and placed in the living room. After the holidays, when it was time to take it down, Doc asked, "Stella, this is so beautiful, can't we keep it up all year?"

Not only was it kept up but also it was decorated for every holiday. She got so much pleasure out of seeing the tree decorated with eggs and Easter bunnies at Easter, flags for the July 4, and appropriate seasonal decorations for all occasions. It kept her aware of the season and helped her look forward to the approaching holiday. A pleasant and peaceful environment made her days much more enjoyable.

Stella's daily visits enabled Elena to go shopping, which she enjoyed, or to simply get outside for a change of pace. Every two weeks, when Stella took Doc to see her sister at the nursing home, Elena would make sure that Doc was in clean and pressed clothes and looking good. Doc appeared healthier and definitely in a good frame of mind.

One evening in June, when everything was on an even keel, Doc stood up, and complained, "Ouch, my left knee is very painful." Stella, who was visiting, could see that she was unable to support her weight. Leaning against the wall Doc tried to give herself extra support but to no avail. "Stella, I can't stand." "Hold on Doc, lets ease you down to the floor so you don't fall." Helping her into a sitting position seemed to exacerbate the pain so Stella had Elena call 911 for emergency help. She was transported to the hospital where they made a diagnosis of a spontaneous fracture of the femur above the left prosthetic knee. The prognosis was grim because the fracture was so extensive it was doubtful that a knee replacement could be accomplished. The attending orthopedic physician gave little hope saying, "Our choices here are not good ones. We could amputate the limb or do nothing and have her remain immobile for the rest of her life." Stella was thrown for a loop with what they presented as choices. Tightening her mouth, she placed a hand over her heart and was beginning to protest that whole situation when Doc's personal physician, Dr. Pilano, appeared and offered a glimmer of hope telling Stella, "There is an orthopedic physician at another hospital that might be willing to attempt a repair on Doc's knee." "Can you call him and ask if he can evaluate Doc today?" Stella said in earnest. "That I can do."

The attending Doctor seemed to be relieved that he would not have to help them make a devastating choice. Doc was transferred to the hospital where the orthopedic surgeon determined that a long prosthesis could be inserted. Surgery was scheduled, but Stella knowing that Doc had both of her knees replaced at approximately the same time many years ago, suspected that the right knee may have a similar fracture. She asked to speak with the resident orthopedic physician. "Doctor, before I sign for Doc's surgery I am requesting that the that the right knee also be evaluated for fracture by x-ray." The physician was not happy with Stella's request saying it was unnecessary. "Doctor, I am Doc's legal guardian and I will not sign for her procedure without a full evaluation of her other knee." Much to the physician's surprise, the right femur was likewise fractured. Surgery was to proceed on one knee to be followed in another week on the other knee. Stella pleaded with the surgeon to try and repair both knees simultaneously. She explained Doc's circumstances and her concern over the two exhausting surgeries would have on Doc. He said he would only if she tolerated the procedure well. Once again, God took mercy on Doc and the procedure went well.

During Doc's hospitalization, Jackie drove out to be with her good friend. Her support and encouragement surely helped Doc in her recovery. Jackie stayed until Doc was discharged to home.

Much to everyone's surprise, Doc regained full mobility and a range of motion even better then her pre-surgical status. Within months, she was walking, with the aid of a walker but free of pain. Her tenacity continued when any obstacle appeared. While Doc was homebound her nephew Phil brought Rita for a visit. Stella was sure Rita begged him to take her to visit Doc. This was the first time that Elena had any contact with Doc's family other than Rita, and took the opportunity to engage in conversation with Phil and asked, "Please tell me about Doc's and your family." He struggled with the answer but finally said, "We're a close-knit family and all get along really well" Elena not one to mince words said quickly, "I don't think you are very close as Doc has been home for eleven months, and this is the first visit from her family." Phil didn't have much to say after that. "Having a family close to share in good times and bad is important in everyone's life. It seems that Stella and her children are more of a family to Doc than yours."

Following this visit, Doc began to experience a gradual decline in health and one day passed out while on the toilet and was taken to the hospital. A diagnosis of dehydration was made and she was treated with fluids and released. This occurred again about ten days later and while in the emergency room, the staff was having difficulty in finding a good vein from which to draw blood. They attempted many times and Stella saw the discomfort that this caused her friend, prompting her to call Dr. Pilano. "Doctor, we are here at the emergency room and the staff is attempting to draw her blood. It's really become very difficult and I wonder if all of this is actually necessary." What are we talking about Stella, do you think it is time to place Doc into in home hospice program?" There was silence for a moment and then Stella made an important decision for her friend. Stella, being a nurse, was aware of hospice benefits. "Yes, I think it is time. Why shouldn't we make her life as comfortable as possible? Nothing, no amount of blood tests is going to extend her life, so, yes, let's do that." Her physician agreed that it would be prudent to do so" "I will come to the hospital to see Doc and evaluate her for hospice."

From that moment on, a flock of angels appeared on their doorstep. Doc would no longer have to endure hospitalizations and excessive testing but would be in her home receiving comforting care, beginning with a physician assessment. A nurse came to review all medications and left pain-control medications, explaining what to give and when to give these special drugs. The hospice team gave personal support to Doc's caretaker and Stella. In addition, an aide came twice weekly to bathe Doc. A minister visited and prayed with Doc. Hospice was great in assisting Doc as she neared the end of her life. Their goal was to assist the family in caring for Doc by making her as comfortable as possible, ultimately improving her quality of life.

As her dementia progressed, she was not brushing her teeth very well and so Stella purchased an electric toothbrush to assist her in brushing her teeth. If she resisted, Stella only had to remind her of how beautiful her teeth were and Doc would smile widely and let her brush away.

Stella and Elena stuck to a routine whenever possible. Every evening a few hours before Doc's bedtime Stella would come over and spend time with Doc. At bedtime more often than not, Doc would want to stay up longer. Stella would tell her that she had to be home within a short time and if Doc didn't go to bed at that time, Stella wouldn't be able to help her. This always worked.

At bedtime, Stella played recordings of Doc's favorite classical music. She would give her a gentle massage. The music coupled with a massage seemed to soothe Doc. Afterwards, they would talk for a while and as Doc tired, Stella would leave the room and tell her to dream of angels.

In November, suddenly, the ability for Doc to talk with her sister by phone stopped. Doc was agitated and continually asked, "Can we call Rita please?" After five days, Doc and Stella became concerned. A phone call to the nursing home administration office informed them that Rita was no longer a resident there and that they could not provide any information per the family's directive. Phone calls were made to various nursing homes. Checking the obituaries online gave Stella no relevant information other than knowing Rita was still alive. About ten days later, Doc became suddenly ill and efforts to locate Rita were accelerated. Stella and her friends called every nursing home and hospital within a thirty-mile radius. They were on a mission and vowed to locate Rita. Stella found a patient with the last name of Sliwa at a hospital (one where Jean was on staff) and proceeded to phone her, but each time someone answered when asked if she was Rita, the woman said no. Undaunted, Stella swore that she could hear Jean's voice in the background, still the woman said no. Stella was crazed and convinced that because of the unique last name of Doc and Rita, it had to be her. She enlisted the help of a friend and they traveled to the hospital, but Stella was reluctant to go inside, fearing an altercation with Rita's family. Her friend felt no such reluctance and proudly marched into the hospital and up to the floor housing Rita. Speaking to the nurses at the nursing desk, she loudly decried the efforts of a physician who would shamefully hide her aunt, even going to the degree of changing her first name. Without further ado, she flounced down to the patient room, threw back the curtain, calling out Rita's name only to find that it was not Rita but indeed another woman. Needless to say, her exit from the hospital was less elegant then her entrance. Stella would often look back on this, chuckle, and wonder what that poor woman thought, having a crazed lady call her three days in a row insisting that she was Rita and then have a total stranger enter her room, also calling her

Rita. Stella and friends changed their approach when calling facilities from asking if a Rita Sliwa was a resident to asking to speak with Rita. Bingo, their efforts were finally rewarded and they located her. The next day, Stella and two friends drove out to see Rita and she was so happy to see them. Rita said "When Jean brought me here she said she misplaced my phonebook and that's why I couldn't let you know where I was. I was so worried about my sister" Rita applauded Stella saying, "You are better than a private detective. All of my family thinks so."

One weekend, when Stella was watching Doc, Sam, who was Doc's friend and Stella's brother-in-law, walked over to visit with her. Sam, who also was in declining health, had not visited for several weeks. They sat holding hands and talking, and Stella felt that these two friends were saying a final goodbye to one another. Stella recalled this as a beautiful scene of love. That evening about an hour after getting her ready for bed, Doc cried out in severe pain. Stella administered the suggested drugs but there was not the expected relief. As Doc continued crying out in pain, Stella called the hospice emergency number and asked what she could do. The hospice nurse came to see Doc and suggested she be placed in the inpatient hospice unit for pain control. An ambulance was called and Doc was transported.

Doc always took excellent care of her teeth and was proud that people thought they were dentures because they were so perfect. While in the inpatient hospice unit, Stella observed that no one was brushing her teeth and asked the staff to be more diligent and brush them. When Stella visited the next day, Doc's nurse was laughing as she told Stella "We were pulling on Doc's teeth, thinking they were dentures when Doc who was hardly responding due to pain medication, clearly yelled, they are mine"

Two of Stella's friends came to visit Doc and spent time singing Christmas carols with her and just being there, telling her how much they loved her. One friend took Stella aside and advised her to take Doc home, insisting that she shouldn't meet her maker in a hospital but at home. It was because of this advice that Stella asked to release Doc, as the pain now was under control.

While Doc was still hospitalized Vic called to inform Stella that a court date had been set regarding the petition filed to require Jean to make restitution for Doc's missing personal items. Recognizing that Doc was dying Stella decided it was no longer important and told Vic not to proceed.

For an additional two weeks, she rested peacefully in her own home, where she had spent her last two years surrounded by wonderful memories and caring friends. On occasion, especially during the night, Stella or Elena would hear Doc talking to someone. Stella asked, "Who are you talking to, is it your mother, other family members or God?" Doc would just answer, "Sometimes."

One night while sitting by Doc's bed, Stella took her hand and told her everything she wanted her to know, starting with how thankful she was that Doc chose her to be her friend.

"You have made me a better person by knowing and observing you and your goodness and I thank you. It's okay to leave this world Doc, your family and many friends who have gone before you are waiting, so don't worry about me, I will be fine with the memories of you fresh in my mind."

When Doc would occasionally verbalize that she was a burden to everyone, she would quickly be reminded of all she did for others and assured that she was a blessing to all. Everyone felt lucky to have had her in his or her lives. She was loved and cared for at the end of her life, allowing her to die with dignity. Her legacy to all should be of strength and faith. Doc returned to her heavenly father breathing her last breath rosary in-hand and her best friend at her side.

"Not how long, but how well you have lived is the main thing,"
> *Seneca*

Stella found fulfillment in viewing each day not as a duty or hardship but rather as a gift of being able to help someone who needed care in her last years of life. The joy and satisfaction she derived from this experience far exceeded the giving. For this opportunity, Stella was and will be eternally grateful.

"The greatest gift of life is friendship and I have received it."
> *Hubert Humphrey*

The End

www.ingramcontent.com/pod-product-compliance
Lightning Source LLC
Chambersburg PA
CBHW030211130726
47898CB00012B/969